Victoria Torres, Unfortunately Average
is published by Stone Arch Books,
A Capstone Imprint
1710 Roe Crest Drive
North Mankato, Minnesota 56003
www.mycapstone.com

Cataloging-in-Publication Data is available on the Library of Congress website.

ISBN: 978-1-4965-3818-5 (library binding)
ISBN: 978-1-4965-3820-8 (paperback)
ISBN: 978-1-4965-3826-0 (eBook PDF)

Summary: It's summertime and that means softball season! Victoria Torres is joining up
with some of her friends to play coed softball on a city-league team coached by none
other than her dad. As an experienced pitcher, Vicka thinks this is her chance to shine on
the mound. But her dad has different plans. He wants her and her strong arm in center
field, but Victoria hates being stuck in the outfield! How will she deal with this curveball?

Designer: Bobbie Nuytten
Image credits: Photographs by Shutterstock: arttonick, 156 (ice cream), Elnur, cover
(bats), Mejini Neskah, cover (ball and glove), Phovoir, cover (cap), Pretty Vectors, cover
(chihuahua illustration); Line drawings by Capstone: Sandra D'Antonio and Shutterstock

Printed and bound in Canada.
10048S17FR

CURVEBALL

by Julie Bowe

STONE ARCH BOOKS
a capstone imprint

All About Me

Hi, I'm Victoria Torres — Vicka for short. Not that I am short. Or tall. I'm right in the middle, otherwise known as "average height for my age." I'm almost twelve years old and just started sixth grade at Middleton Middle School. My older sister, Sofia, is an eighth grader. My little brother, Lucas, is in kindergarten, so that puts me in the middle of my family too:

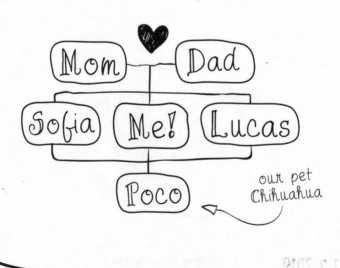

Mom — Dad

Sofia — Me! — Lucas

Poco ← our pet Chihuahua

DEC 1 3 2019

I'm average in other ways too. I live in a middle-sized house at the center of an average town. I get Bs for grades, sit in the middle of the flute section in band, and can hit a baseball only as far as the shortstop. And even though she would say I'm "above average," I'm not always the BEST best friend to my BFF, Bea.

Still, my parents did name me Victoria — as in victory? They had high hopes for me right from the start! This year, I am determined to be better than average in every way!

 Me!

Chapter 1

Play Ball!

"Oooo . . . Vicka! Listen to this song. It's called 'Centerfield.'" My best friend, Bea, pops out one of her earbuds and wiggles it into my ear. She's been putting together a playlist of softball music so we can rock, on and off the softball field, this summer. We're sitting on my front steps, waiting for our other BFF, Jenny, to show up so we can all bike to the Middleton Community Center together. That's where registration for the summer softball league is happening later today.

I listen to the song blasting from Bea's music player. She has the other bud in her ear, singing along with the upbeat tune pounding against our eardrums. "Put me in coach. I'm ready to play . . . today!" The song is super fast and fun! It's sure to get us jazzed up and ready to play before each game this summer.

Jenny has played on softball teams since she was in grade school. Bea and I have never played on an actual team, but Jenny talked us into signing up this year. I've got all my fingers and toes crossed, hoping we all get put on the same team!

Annelise, Katie, Grace, and Julia from our class are trying out too, along with some other girls. I heard some of the boys will be playing too. All the softball teams are coed, which means girls and boys play together. Jenny's mom, Mrs. Jackson, is in charge of the whole program. She's way into sports, just like Jenny! If I can have her as my coach and my besties as my teammates, my summer will totally shine!

Just because I haven't played organized sports doesn't mean I'm a total newbie. At our last Torres family picnic, us kids challenged the grown-ups to a game of softball. I got to pitch, and my team won! Afterward, Dad told me I was a natural, which made me feel fantabulous because his opinion means a lot to me. He and my uncle, Julio, played on a baseball team in college. Dad even won a trophy for being the MVP — Most Valuable Player!

I know I'm not as good a player as Jenny and some of my other classmates, but if I could pitch for a Middleton team this summer, then I could really step up to the plate and show what I'm made of. I would be Victoria Torres, star of the team!

"Here comes Jenny," Bea says, looking down the block.

"What'd you say?" I ask, coming out of my field-of-dreams daze.

Bea plucks out my earbud. "I said, Jenny is here! Grab my bike for me, will you? I have to finish downloading another song."

I hop up and wheel our bikes over from the driveway. The more I think about playing on a team this summer, the more I think softball might really be my way to finally shine!

"Hey, you two!" Jenny calls out, biking up the walk. "Ready to play ball?"

"*I* am," I reply. "But Bea is still trying to make the perfect playlist."

"What's wrong with that?" Bea asks, rushing to tuck away her music player. "I'll need something to listen to while I'm counting dandelions in the outfield!"

Jenny laughs. "Not me," she says. "I plan to play shortstop or first base. The only thing *I'll* be counting are the number of runners I get out!"

I smile at Jenny. "And I'll be counting the number of batters I *strike* out!"

Bea hops on her bike. "I never knew softball had so much math in it." She giggles, then pushes off and starts pedaling down the block. "Come on!" she calls to us over her shoulder. "It's time to play ball!"

When we pedal up to the community center a few minutes later, lots of kids and parents are arriving to register. We park our bikes near the big sign that's taped up next to the entrance and hurry inside.

Some of the boys from our class — Sam, Henry, Drew, and Ed — are sitting at a table just inside the entrance. Secretly, I'm crushing on Drew, but he doesn't know it. Bea, Jenny, and I are friends with all the boys, even though they can act like total goofballs when they get together.

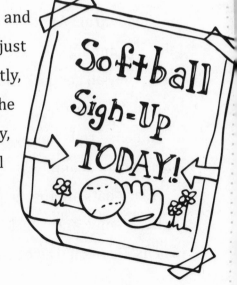

Right now, Henry is using a pencil like a softball bat, hitting crumpled-up paper balls across the table while Drew, Sam, and Ed use their fingers to run around an imaginary softball diamond.

"Bases loaded!" Henry calls out as he tosses up another paper ball and whacks it with the pencil. The paper ball sails across the aisle and bonks Annelise in the head! She's sitting at another table with some other girls.

"Watch it!" she snaps, whipping the ball back at the boys. It flies past them and drops to the floor.

"Good arm, Annelise!" Henry yells. His fingers take off running the bases along with the other boys. When they all get back to home plate, they pretend to body slam their fingers.

Annelise rolls her eyes. "They better not put you jokers on *my* team."

Henry bats another paper ball at her.

Bea, Jenny, and I pick up registration forms and pencils, then join the other girls at their table. Katie,

Grace, and Julia are sitting with Annelise, filling out forms too. After we all say hi, I notice Annelise is using a light-up gel pen with a sparkly pink pom-pom decorating the end of it. Each time she writes, a bright pink light blinks inside the pen. She must have brought the pen from home. Annelise likes to do everything with a lot of flare, even when she's just writing her name.

As I sit down, I see Dad and Uncle Julio talking with some of the other sponsors at the front of the room, including Mrs. Jane. She owns *Java Jane's*, a coffee shop in town where my friends and I like to hang out. Julia's parents are there too — they own the greenhouse in town. I'm super proud that my family's music store, The Middle Si, is one of the league's sponsors. Each year, the sponsors provide team shirts and baseball caps for all the players on each team.

I look over my registration form and start filling in the blanks . . . it's all easy stuff like name, address, and email. In the space that asks about past softball experience, I write about playing at school and with my family. When I get to the last question on the page, I smile.

In big, bold letters I write my answer:

PITCHER

Glancing around the table, I see that Bea is writing *Outfielder* for her favorite position. Jenny has written *First base or Shortstop*. I can't see what Katie, Grace, and Julia are writing, but Annelise's answer is easy to see because of her bright pink pen. She's even drawing artsy exclamation points after her answer.

PITCHER!!!

I grip my pencil tighter than a softball bat. *Annelise wants to pitch too?* I shouldn't be surprised. Lately, it seems like she and I are always competing over the same things. At school this past year, we both tried out for the cheerleading squad, then we both ran for class president, and also auditioned for the lead in our class play. Now we both want to pitch? *¡Uf!*

I glance around the packed room. Lots of kids are here to play softball. There will probably be a dozen different teams. Chances are Annelise will be assigned to one of the other teams, not mine . . . right?

I look at Annelise again. Now she's drawing stars around her answer!

I turn back to *my* answer. Then I draw a few exclamation points and stars too, just to be safe.

"Good evening, everyone!" Jenny's mom says, stepping up to a microphone and greeting the crowd. "Welcome to summer softball registration! I want to begin by thanking all the Middleton businesses that will be sponsoring our teams this year. Their generous financial support makes our league possible. Will the sponsors please stand?"

A bunch of adults get up from their chairs, including Dad and Uncle Julio! Everyone applauds. I clap the loudest of all.

"We will have a brief sponsors' meeting following registration," Jenny's mom says as the applause dies down. "Sponsors will choose their team name and color. This year, the league board has decided to go with dog names for all the teams!"

"Woof!" Henry barks.

Everyone laughs.

Bea, Jenny, and I look at each other, then bounce in our chairs. Dog names will be fun! I wonder which kind of dog we'll get for our team? The Bulldogs? The Dalmatians?? The German Shepherds??? They all sound like winning names to me. And I'm crossing my fingers and toes hoping that my team's color will be my favorite — lime green! Lately, Bea, Jenny, and I have been going ape over that color. If we're lucky, we will be playing for the Lime Green Labradors! With a name like that, my team is sure to win from the first pitch of the season!

"Coaches will also meet after registration to set up the teams," Jenny's mom continues. "Players, your coaches will contact you within the next few days. Parents, we are still looking for a few more coaches. Please talk to me after the meeting if you'd like to volunteer. Practices will begin at the end of the week. Games will follow shortly thereafter. Let's make this our best season yet! Play ball!"

Everyone applauds again. As we turn in our registration forms, Dad gives me a wave from where he's sitting with the other sponsors. I give him a big smile and wave back. Maybe he'll know which team I'm on later tonight! I *triple* cross my fingers and toes that I will be on a top-dog team, like the Greyhounds or the Rottweilers. Even an unfortunately average girl likes to show her teeth now and then!

Chapter 2

Coach Dad

When I hear Dad pull into our driveway later that night, I dash to the kitchen like I'm trying to steal second base. My dog, Poco, almost gets trampled as I burst through the doorway. Poco is a tiny Chihuahua, so it's easy to miss seeing him when I'm in a hurry. Fortunately, he jumps out of the way before he gets smooshed.

"Sorry, Poco!" I say, skidding to a stop and scooping up my little dog. "I didn't see you there! I'm in a hurry to find out which softball team I'll be playing on!"

Poco yips excitedly and licks my cheek. He is always quick to forgive and forget. Even though he is small enough to fit inside my backpack, I think it takes a pretty big dog to do that!

Tucking Poco under my arm, I race to the back door and pull it open just as Dad is coming inside. "*Hola*, Bonita!" he says, calling me by the nickname he gave me when I was a baby. "So nice of you to open the door for your old man!"

Dad stoops over like he has an achy back. Sometimes he goofs around as much as the boys from my class. It must be a guy thing.

I ignore Dad's old-man routine and hover around him like a hummingbird. "Did the coaches pick teams tonight? Do you know which one I'm on? Am I with Bea? And Jenny? Did we get a good coach? What color is my team shirt? What's my team name? Is it the Dobermans or the —"

Dad throws his hands into the air. "*¡Me doy por vencido!*" he cries, which is Spanish for "I give up!"

Poco lets out a yelp and squirms in my arms. I must be squeezing him too tightly in my excitement. I let him jump down and dash to the safety of his doggie bed in the corner of the kitchen.

Then I turn back to Dad. I have to know which team I will be playing on and if I'll be winning games with my BFFs! "Which team am I on, *por favor*?" I ask Dad politely.

Dad smiles and sets down the folder he's carrying. It has the Middleton Softball League logo on the cover. "You'll be playing on the same team as Bea," Dad tells me.

I squeal like a very happy piglet. "Is Jenny on our team too?"

Dad shakes his head. "Sorry, but Jenny will be playing on her mom's team. Some other girls from your class will be playing with you, though."

My shoulders slump a little. "I was really hoping to be on a team with *both* of my best friends. And I was hoping to have Jenny's mom as *my* coach."

Dad pats my shoulder. "I hope you'll be happy to know you're on *my* team. Our store is the sponsor!"

I gasp. "Our store is sponsoring *my* team?!"

"*¡Si!*" Dad replies, nodding. "And not only that, but . . ."

I start doing my piglet impersonation again. How cool is it that my family is sponsoring my very own team! "What color will our shirts be? Which dog name did we get? Who is my coach?"

Dad holds up his hands again, so I lock my lips and try to stand still. But it's hard to keep quiet when so many questions are bouncing around inside me.

"When I said you're on *my* team, I meant more than just the music shop," Dad says.

I give Dad a puzzled look. "What do you mean more than just the music shop?" I repeat.

Dad goes to the refrigerator and takes out a pitcher of juice. Pouring himself a glass, he says, "The league was still short a couple coaches, so I volunteered to coach a team. *Your* team, to be exact."

My jaw practically drops to my lime green sneakers. "*You're* my coach?"

Dad nods. "I thought it would be a great way for us to spend time together this summer! Now that you're in middle school, I hardly see you anymore."

That's true. Ever since I started middle school, I've been extra busy with classes and activities with my friends. I can't remember the last time Dad and I did something together, just the two of us.

I give Dad a big smile. Then I give him a ginormous hug. "It will be fun having you as my coach! I can become the best pitcher ever with you in my corner."

"Pitcher, huh?" Dad says, hugging me back. "I'm glad you're happy about me being your coach, Bonita. Together, we'll make the Pink Chihuahuas the best team in the league!"

Taking a step back, I stare at Dad. "D-Did you say our team name is the . . . the . . . *Pink Chihuahuas*?"

Dad grins from ear to ear. "I knew you'd love it!" he says. "Poco can be our team mascot. I'll even order a tiny team shirt, just for him! I chose pink especially for you. I know it's your favorite color!"

Dad tousles my hair, then picks up his softball folder and juice and goes looking for Mom.

I just stand there, frozen like a girl-sized Popsicle in the middle of our kitchen. *Dad still thinks my favorite color is pink?* I haven't liked pink best since fifth grade. *My team name is the Chihuahuas?* I love Poco, but Chihuahuas are one of the tiniest dogs in the world. How can we be the *best* team with a little name like that?

I cringe, wondering who else, besides Bea, is going to be a Chihuahua. Will the rest of my teammates think it's a wimpy name and babyish color too? *And what will they think of my dad being our coach?* I wonder, picking up Poco from his little bed and carrying him upstairs with me. Dad chose pink because he thought it was my favorite color. Will my teammates think I'm getting special treatment because I'm his daughter?

When I get to my room, I flop down on my bed, thinking things through. Poco settles in next to me and curls into a tiny ball. "On the other hand, Dad already knows I'm a good player," I say, scratching Poco behind his ears. "And he knows I love to pitch. With him as my coach, I'm sure to lead my team to victory from the pitcher's mound!"

Chapter 3

Jenny the Frenemy

"I think it's a cute team name, and our team color is pinkalicious!" Bea exclaims when I meet up with her at the city pool the next day. We're on our beach towels under one of the poolside umbrellas, talking about the Pink Chihuahuas. Dad called all the players last night to tell them that he will be their coach and that our first practice will be tomorrow afternoon.

"But are you sure *everyone* will like my dad's choices?" I ask. "He showed me the roster earlier. Sam, Henry, Drew, and Ed are on our team. What if they toss Poco around like a softball? And change our name to the Putrid Pink Chihuahuas instead?"

Bea shakes her head. "They won't. Poco is fierce! Not to mention übercute. No one will toss him anywhere. And who doesn't like pink? Even the guys are into it."

That's true. Lots of guys from our school are wearing pink these days. And Bea is right about Poco. He may be tiny on the outside, but he has the heart of a German shepherd! I give my BFF a relieved smile. Bea always has a way of looking on the bright side and helping me see things from a different angle.

"The guys will be thankful just to be on a team with such cool girls," Bea continues, fluffing up her hair in a cool-girl way. We giggle together, then she adds, "Plus, *Drew* will be doubly thankful, because he gets to be on a team with *you*." Now her eyes sparkle with mischief.

Bea knows I'm crushing on Drew, and she loves to tease me about it. She glances toward the diving board where he's waiting his turn to jump off, after Henry.

"Look out below!" Henry shouts from high above the pool, then cannonballs into the water.

"Stop it, Bea," I say, even though I like it when we tease each other in a friendly way. "I won't have time for crushes if I'm going to be the best pitcher in the league. From here on out, pitching is my life."

Bea takes out a tube of sunscreen and starts slathering some on. "And the outfield will be *my* life. Who else is on our team, by the way?" she asks.

"Julia . . . Min . . . and unfortunately, Annelise . . ."

Bea freezes, a glob of sunscreen on her nose. "Seriously? Annelise is on our team?"

I nod. "And you know she wants to be pitcher too. Seems like I'm always competing with her," I say.

Bea sighs, rubbing in the lotion. "Why do we always get stuck doing stuff with her?"

I shrug. "Bad luck? I wish she and Jenny could switch. But Jenny is assigned to the Blue Huskies, her mom's team. Last summer, Mrs. Jackson's team was undefeated!"

Bea cringes. "Um . . . your dad has coached softball before . . . right?" she asks.

I fiddle nervously with my lime green sunglasses, then put them on. "Not that I know of. But he was the star of his baseball team!"

"Which team?" Bea asks.

I shrug. "I'm not sure. It was back when he was in college."

"College?" Bea says. "We weren't even born yet!"

Now *I* cringe.

But Bea brushes off her doubts in the twinkle of an eye. "I'm sure your dad will be a great coach," she says in her upbeat way. Then she tosses aside the sunscreen and pops in her earbuds. Lying back on her beach towel she says, "I've added more songs to my softball playlist." She bops her foot in time to the beat under our shady umbrella. "I can jam for at least seven innings in the outfield!"

"And hopefully I'll be pitching for each one," I add. In the back of my mind, I'm wondering what kind of skills Annelise might have, but I have to think posi-tive. Leaning back, I close my eyes, imagining myself standing on the pitcher's mound with a crowd of fans cheering my name.

"Vicka! Yoo-hoo, Vicka!"

I open my eyes with a start, realizing it's not the crowd shouting my name. It's Annelise.

¡Uf!

Annelise flip-flops up to Bea and me in her bright pink cover up. Julia is at her heels.

"Hi there, teamies!" she says to us. "I've been looking for you everywhere!" She spreads out her beach towel and sits down. "Now that we are team-mates, we should hang out together."

I look to Bea for backup, but she's zoning out to her tunes.

"Vicka, your dad called me last night to *person-ally* tell me how happy he is to have me on his team," Annelise continues. "Sit down, Julia, you're blocking my rays."

Julia scoots in next to Annelise.

I roll my eyes behind my lime green shades. "My dad called everyone on the team, Annelise, not just you," I tell her.

Annelise stretches out her tan legs. "Well, he called me *first*," she says.

Julia stretches out her legs too. Even though Julia is the same age as us, she's way taller — and way less bossy than Annelise. "I'm super excited to be on a team with you and Bea," she tells me.

I reach over and give Julia a high five. "Go, Chihuahuas!" we shout together.

"Katie and Grace are playing for those *awful* Blue Huskies," Annelise says, pulling a pair of pink shades from her beach bag.

"That's not awful," I say. "Jenny is a Husky too."

Annelise makes a face like she's sucking on a sour apple jawbreaker. "Like I said . . . *awful*." Annelise and Jenny have never gotten along very well. "But never mind, we'll beat the tails off those Huskies," she continues. "Coach Torres was so happy to hear what a great pitcher I am. He's counting on me to lead our team to victory."

I frown. "My dad said that?"

Annelise nods and takes off her cover-up. Her one-piece is bright pink too and sparkles like a crown. "He basically said he can't win without me!" she says, before popping in her earbuds.

As Annelise digs through her beach bag for snacks, I stiffen like a piece of driftwood on my beach towel. Did Dad really say that or is Annelise bragging again? He knows I'm good at pitching. I even wrote pitcher as my top choice on my registration form.

"Ignore her," Bea says under her breath. She pops out an earbud and looks at me. I guess she could hear Annelise's braggy voice over her private jam session. "You know how she's always putting herself in the spotlight."

I nod, relieved to hear Bea say that and amazed that she knew just what I was thinking. Sometimes best friends don't need words to know what's on your mind.

Unfortunately, I'm not feeling as confident as my BFF. I love my dad, and he is a lot of fun. But can he coach someone like Annelise without letting her take over the team? I guess I'll find out, starting tomorrow, when we have our first practice. For now, there's nothing to do but doggie-paddle around the pool and soak up some summer fun before we get to work, throwing and hitting and, most of all, pitching.

Just then I see Jenny getting in line at the concession stand. "Hey, let's see if Jenny wants to swim with us!" I say to the other girls.

But Annelise grabs my arm as I start to stand up. "No swimming with the frenemy," she says.

"Frenemy?!" I gawk at Annelise. "Jenny is one of our best friends!"

"The team comes first," Annelise snips. "I had to ditch Katie and Grace for the summer too. Your friendship with Jenny is on hold until after our game against the Huskies."

I wag my head like Annelise is speaking French poodle. "You're crazy if you think I'm ditching Jenny for the summer. I can be her friend *and* play against her in softball, Annelise."

But Annelise doesn't budge. "You can't expect to beat the cleats off the Huskies if you're sharing Popsicles with their star player."

As Annelise starts pushing juice pouches and candy bars into our hands, I look back toward the concession stand and watch Jenny melt into the crowd.

Chapter 4

Team Chihuahua!

I'm halfway between nervous and excited as Bea, Jenny, and I pedal our bikes to the practice fields behind Middleton Middle School the next afternoon. Other teams are already there, warming up in the batting cages and tossing softballs back and forth across the grassy outfield.

"There's my team!" Jenny says, turning her bike toward one of the practice fields. "See you later!"

"Bye!" Bea calls after her.

"Later!" I chime in.

Bea and I head to the diamond at the far end of the field where Dad told us to meet. Sam, Drew, Henry, and Ed are there playing catch. When they see us bike up to the third-base fence line, Drew chucks the ball to Henry, then gives us a wave.

"Hi, you two!" he calls out, walking up to the fence. "Cool about your dad being our coach, Vicka."

I try to act casual, as though he's just any boy, not my crush, talking to me. I unhook my glove from my bike rack and walk over to the fence, trying not to trip in my cleats. Bea told me I should wait to put them on when we got here. I should have listened to her.

"Yeah, it's pretty cool," I reply, even though I'm still worried the other kids might not agree. At least Drew seems to think Dad coaching is a good thing. "But I wish he would have picked a better dog name. I mean, wouldn't you rather play for a team like the Huskies or the Dobermans?"

"Nope," Drew says, not missing a beat. "Why would I want to be a Husky when I can be a Chihuahua?"

I blink with surprise behind my glasses. "But a husky could eat two Chihuahuas for breakfast!"

Drew laughs. "Small is good," he says. "It makes us the underdogs, which means we've got more to prove than the others. And that will make us work harder to beat them."

As Drew looks around at the other teams playing ball on their practice fields, I glance at Bea to see if she has noticed that I am chatting with my crush. But she's busy fussing with her music player again.

"And when we do win," Drew says, turning back to me, "it will make it that much sweeter! I'd rather work my tail off for each win than strut around as top dog with nowhere to go but down."

I nod. What Drew said makes a lot of sense. Playing hard and entertaining our fans are my goals too. But now that I see more of my teammates arriving, I feel more and more responsible for making our team shine because my dad is our coach.

Secretly, these past few days, I've been feeling afraid that he might mess up. Last night I heard him complaining to Mom about his achy shoulder. And this morning he admitted to Lucas that the last time he hit a ball out of the park he was still wearing braces on his teeth. Shouldn't coaches be in good shape and be pros at hitting home runs?

When I was a little kid, Dad was a superhero to me. Now that I'm older, I sometimes see him for who he really is, which isn't always perfect. Sometimes he does stuff that makes me act like I don't even know who he is.

Last week at the mall, he let Lucas take a ride on one of those mechanical cars they have at the arcade. The car jiggles up and down when you put a couple coins in it. That wasn't so bad, because Lucas is still a little kid. But then my dad climbed onto the mechanical airplane and took a ride too! Lucas thought it was the greatest thing in the world, but I wanted to dive into my jumbo blue slushie and disappear! Instead, I ducked behind a pinball machine and hid there until their rides came to an end.

At least there are no kiddie rides at the practice fields. And I know Dad was an MVP. But that was a long time ago. Does he have what it takes to be an MVC — Most Valuable Coach?

Just then, a red sports car zips up to our practice field. Annelise hops out and waves goodbye to her dad. I've never seen the car before, but it's no surprise. Her parents are both rich. She was bragging to us at the pool yesterday that her dad just bought a new house with its own pool in the backyard so we should be grateful she was swimming with us at all.

"Er . . . gotta go," Drew says when he sees Annelise.

"Chicken," I tease, because we all try to avoid her most days.

"Bawk, bawk!" Drew clucks, then hurries back to the guys.

Annelise runs toward me with a huge smile on her face. Seriously, if she smiled any bigger her teeth would fall out of her mouth! Her whole outfit — baseball cap, shirt, shorts, socks, and cleats — is bright pink. As she gets closer, I see a picture of a softball diamond on her shirt. *Queen of Diamonds* is printed on it.

"Make way for the queen," I say, glancing at Bea again. But she's still plugged into her tunes and doesn't hear me.

A moment later, Annelise is hugging me tighter than a teddy bear. "Thank you, thank you, thank you, Vicka!" she cries.

"For what?" I ask, squirming out of her grip.

"For getting your dad to choose *pink* for our team color!" she exclaims. "I went to the mall last night and bought this most excellent softball outfit at the sports shop! I'll wear it for all of our games!" Annelise strikes a movie-star pose.

"It's called a uniform, not an outfit," I tell her. "And our sponsor provides us with hats and shirts to wear for our games, so we all match." I zero in on her Queen of Diamonds shirt. "Or were you planning to wear a *crown* for our games instead of a cap?"

Annelise squints at my crown comment. "Very funny," she sasses.

I hide a snicker. "Even Poco gets to wear a pink uniform. But I didn't pick the color. My dad ... I mean, Coach Torres did." I decide not to mention that Dad thought pink was still my favorite color.

"Who's Poco?" Annelise asks, glancing around at the other kids, tossing softballs back and forth. "Some new boy?"

I shake my head. "Poco is my pet Chihuahua."

Bea pops out an earbud. "And our team mascot!" She can multitask when she wants to, listening to music and girls gabbing at the same time.

"Hey, that's cool," Henry says. He's standing by the fence line now, along with the other guys. They can never resist snooping into our conversations for long.

"Mascots are good luck! We're going to need all the luck we can get!"

"Aw, c'mon, Hen," Drew says, punching his buddy in the arm. "We've got what it takes to win with *skill*, not luck."

But looking around at our team so far, I've got to agree with Henry. We could use some good luck. Bea's busy with her playlist. Annelise seems more interested in modeling for a softball fashion magazine than playing the game. Sam and Ed could pass for chipmunks — their cheeks are stuffed with sunflower seeds, and they keep spitting the slimy shells on the ground. And then there's me . . . not sure where I fit in at all.

Henry shakes his head gravely. "I hate to disagree, Drewster, but I saw the Blue Huskies practicing last night. They're practicing again today. They've got a killer team."

"That's the team that Jenny's on," I say. "Her mom is the coach."

Henry nods. "Jenny was in on an amazing double play last night. And can she ever slam the ball!"

"Stop with all the doom and gloom," Annelise says, putting on her pink sunglasses. "You have to *believe* to *achieve*!"

We all roll our eyes as Annelise continues giving us a pep talk.

But she stops short when a van rumbles up to our practice field. *The Middle Si Music Shop* is printed in big letters across the side of the van. Dad gives the van's horn a tap, then waves to us from the driver's seat.

Annelise gasps. "Coach Torres is here! I have *got* to talk to him!"

"End of pep talk," Drew says as Annelise hurries over to Dad.

"I can't say that I'm heartbroken," Ed replies.

Sam and Henry snicker.

"I hope your dad brought earplugs, Vicka," Henry says to me as we watch Annelise hop up and down, jabbering to Dad as he gets out of the van. "He's gonna need them with Annelise playing on his team."

Now everyone is snickering.

I gulp.

The boys go back to playing catch. Bea takes a pair of cleats from her bike rack and sits down to put them on. I watch as Dad pulls a bulky equipment bag from the back of the van. Annelise grabs it from him and hoists it over her skinny shoulder, still talking, as Dad pulls out another bag.

"Just look at her, carrying a bag that's bigger than she is!" I mutter. "We should crown her the queen of the *showoffs*."

Bea glances up from tying her cleats. "Actually, it looks like she's being helpful for once, that's all," she replies.

I shoot a *Huh?* look at Bea. "You know she's only pitching in because she wants to be the star pitcher."

Bea raises her eyebrows. "Are you jealous or something?"

"No! Why would I be jealous?!"

Bea shrugs and grabs her glove. "Because Annelise wants the same thing you do — to shine as the brightest star on our team."

"I don't want to be the *star*, Bea," I say, even though secretly I do. "I just don't want my dad to be duped by her phony act."

"Your dad can handle Annelise," Bea replies, thumping her fist against her glove. "Come on, let's toss the ball around with the boys. I want to tell them about my great playlist!" She adjusts her earbuds, then hurries over to where the boys are playing catch.

". . . and, once, I got an actual *home run* when I was only, like, eight years old!" Annelise is still talking my dad's ear off as they lug the equipment bags to the third-base dugout. "It was just kickball, but so what?

I'm obviously really good at sports. You should totally make me your starting pitcher!"

Dad just nods and smiles.

I frown so hard my glasses slip down a notch on my nose. My heart starts hammering like a paddle-ball against my chest. I can't let my dad fall for her bragging!

Marching over to the dugout, I grab the equipment bag Annelise is carrying. "I'll take that," I say, jerking the bag from her shoulder. It falls to the ground with a loud clatter of bats and balls, nearly squishing Annelise's foot.

"What are you doing?!" Annelise glares at me. "That bag is heavy. You could have broken my toe!"

"I'm *so* sorry," I reply in a not-sorry voice. "I just wanted to *pitch* in . . . like *you*."

Annelise gives me a cool squint. Then she reaches for the bag again. I grab the other end of it. We both pull, like we're playing tug-o-war with a sack of potatoes.

"Girls!" Dad says, breaking up our tugging match. "Save your energy for practice." He takes the bag from us and carries it through the dugout to the infield.

Annelise pushes past me and hurries after Dad. "So can I, Coach Torres?" she asks. "Can I pitch for the team?"

"We'll have to see about that, Annelise," Dad replies. "Remember, every position is important." He shoos Annelise to the outfield to play catch with Bea and the boys.

Phew! Dad didn't give in to her hounding. Good! As soon as practice starts, I'll show everyone that *I've* got what it takes to pitch our team to victory, not Annelise.

Chapter 5

Jump Ropes and Hopscotch?

After everyone arrives for practice, Dad has us circle up on the outfield grass. "Welcome to our first practice, Team Chihuahua!" he says, cheerfully. "You can call me Coach Torres." Dad glances at me and grins. "Except for Vicka. She can call me Dad."

Everyone looks at me.

"*Awww...*" Henry says, making puppy-dog eyes at me. "Coach's pet."

I know Henry is joking around, but I feel my cheeks prickle with heat, and it's not just from the bright sunshine.

"Does this mean Vicka gets out of warm-ups?" Sam asks.

I cringe.

"Not a chance," Dad says. "Everyone is equal on this team, which means we'll all have to work equally hard to win."

When I look up again, everyone is nodding in agreement with Dad. I relax a little. I'm the same as them. We will all have to work hard to prove we are the best.

"First things first," Dad continues, "we can't expect to win if we're not in good shape. We'll start each practice with a run around the ballpark. If you get here early, you might as well start running."

"But, Coach," Ed says, looking around the fence line that circles all the practice fields. "That's gotta be more than a mile!" He already looks out of breath.

"Not even close," Dad replies. "I ran it the other night."

"Coach Torres, you *do* know we're here for soft-ball, not track, right?" Julia asks.

Dad chuckles. "If this were track practice I'd make you run *three* miles. Running is a good way to lim-ber up and get in shape." He looks around the group. His eyes stop on me. For a moment I think he's going to ask me to back him up, but I look away before he can.

Annelise stands up. "You got it, Coach. C'mon Chihuahuas. Get your tails in gear!" She tosses down her pink glove and takes off jogging toward the fence line.

I hear a few grumbles, but soon we all toss aside our gloves and chug along with Annelise.

"My . . . lungs . . . are . . . on . . . fire!" Bea pants as we round the first practice field. Jenny waves to us as we go by.

"Mine . . . too," I reply. It reminds me of when Bea and I tried out for the cheer squad at the start of the last school year. We had to warm up with a run before practice then too. I planned to keep running all year long, but I sort of let that goal slide. Like it or not, it looks like I'm back to getting into shape!

Julia runs up alongside Bea and me. "When do you think we'll get to bat a ball? That's my favorite part."

"I'm sure we'll do that next," I tell Julia, even though I'm not sure at all.

As we tromp down the final stretch, I see Dad taking something from the equipment bag. It doesn't look like a softball bat. It looks more like a rolled up ladder.

What does a ladder have to do with softball? That worried feeling starts to gnaw at my middle again. Does Dad know what he's doing?

By the time we get back to our starting point, Dad has finished rolling out the weird-looking ladder. It's made of flimsy plastic and doesn't look like anything you'd dare climb on.

"Grab some water," Dad tells us as he starts taking bats and balls from one of the equipment bags and setting them aside. "Then we'll start practice."

Finally!

"Do you want me to hand out bats and balls, Dad . . . er . . . I mean, Coach?" I ask, excited to start a real practice.

Truthfully, I'm mostly excited to show everyone my pitching arm. I can already imagine the surprised looks on their faces when I pitch the ball straight through the strike zone. I bet I'll even impress Drew. At the start of the year, I was so gaga over him I could hardly talk to him without blushing and babbling. I still get nervous around him sometimes, but we've gotten to be better friends this year, so the crush thing isn't quite so *crushing*, if you know what I mean.

I start to pick up a few of the bats, but Dad looks up from the equipment bag and shakes his head. "Thanks, Vicka, but we won't be needing the bats and balls quite yet," he says.

"But, Dad," I say in a low voice. "Everyone signed up to play *softball*. My friends want to hit the ball and run the bases!"

Dad smiles patiently. "And so they will! But first we've got to get conditioned." He pats my shoulder. "Trust me, Vicka, I know what I'm doing."

I nod like I believe him, but I bite my lip like I don't.

Dad goes back to the equipment bag. I can't believe my eyes when I see what he pulls out of it.

Jump ropes! Pink, purple, green, orange — just like the ones we played with during recess in grade school. *¡Uf!*

"Oh, goodie!" Henry says, clapping his hands like a preschooler. *"Me want a gween jump wope, pwease!"*

Everyone laughs at Henry's baby talk, even Dad. "We'll throw the ball around a little later, I promise," he says. "First, we need to warm up with some drills."

"Drills?" Ed says. "You mean like power tools, right?"

Dad shakes his head. "I mean like cross jumps and roundabouts." He starts handing out jump ropes to everyone. "Spread out so no one gets tied in knots," he says. "We'll do three sixty-second rounds of jumping. Feel free to switch off from both feet to one foot as you jump. The faster the better! Ready . . . set . . . go!"

Everyone moves out around the dirt infield. Dad times us on a stopwatch he's wearing around his neck as we jump.

"I'm an excellent rope jumper," Annelise brags as she skips lightly over her pink rope. "My mom and I work out at the gym every week." She starts hopping on one foot, then switches to the other foot.

Me? I plod up and down on both feet, counting the seconds until the first minute is up.

"Time!" Dad finally shouts. "Rest for ten seconds, then we'll start round two."

"What's next?" Min pants. "Hopscotch?"

"Looks like it," Julia says, nodding toward the goofy ladder. It does look a little like a hopscotch path.

"Ladder drills, not hopscotch," Henry puts in. "You gotta step in and out of the rungs as fast as you can.

It's good for footwork and reflexes. We had to run ladder drills in wrestling last season."

"Here we go, Chihuahuas!" Dad shouts. "Round two!"

By the time practice is half over, we've done everything except hit a ball or run the bases. My friends and I all collapse on the ground, our legs feeling like giant rubber bands from all the running, jumping, and hopping in and out of ladder rungs.

"Five-minute break," Dad tells us. "Drink some water. Then we'll toss the ball around."

Bea chugs water from her bottle, then falls back on the grass next to me. "Wake me when it's over!" she cries.

Everyone else looks hot and tired too.

I open my water bottle and take a big gulp.

"Don't guzzle it," Annelise tells me. "It will give you stomach cramps."

I take the bottle away from my mouth. "How would you know?" I ask.

Annelise lifts her chin. "It's common knowledge when you exercise as much as I do."

I watch as Annelise sips water from her bright pink water bottle. She's been doing all the drills, same as the rest of us. But, unlike me, she's barely breaking a sweat. A moment later, Annelise hops up and starts stretching out her arms and legs. Then she gets into a pitching stance, windmills her arm, and snaps an invisible ball toward home plate.

"Good form, Annelise!" Dad calls to her as he rolls up the ladder. "Try staggering your feet a bit more. Reach for home plate, then relax your arm as you release the ball."

I wait for Annelise to make a sassy comment to Dad, telling him it's "common knowledge" that her stance is already perfect.

Instead, she nods and says, "Like this, Coach?" Then she repositions her feet and winds up.

"That's it, Annelise!" Dad shouts. "Keep it up!"

Annelise smiles her big, toothy grin, then winds up for another fake pitch . . . and another . . . and another.

I wipe water off my chin and grit my teeth.

Chapter 6

Dog Boy

After dinner that night, I'm still waiting to talk to Dad. He had to go straight to the music store after practice to help Uncle Julio close up for the day, so I didn't have a chance to talk to him then. Mom just got a text saying he is on his way home.

"Please tell your dad there's a plate of leftovers for him in the fridge," Mom tells me. Then she heads upstairs to give Lucas a bath.

I head to the kitchen and wait for Dad to walk in the back door. But unlike last time, I'm not bouncing around with excitement. Instead, I'm standing firm. Dad needs to know he's doing things wrong at practice before things get really bad.

"*Hola*, Victoria!" Dad says as he comes inside a minute later. "Waiting for me again? What a treat. How did you like our first softball practice?"

I'm all prepared to tell Dad the truth — that I didn't like it at all and that Annelise is trying to play favorites so she can rule the team from the pitcher's mound. But now that he's here, face-to-face with me, my courage is bobbling. I don't want to hurt his feelings. After all, he hasn't played on a team for a really long time.

"Practice was okay," I finally say, "but I think everyone would like it better if we actually played softball instead of just running around, getting sweaty and tired."

Dad pats my cheek. "We *are* practicing, Bonita. We can't throw well and run fast with weak arms and legs. Conditioning and getting in shape will carry us a long way this season."

"But my friends didn't sign up to get in shape, Dad," I reply. "They signed up to play softball!"

"And so they will, Vicka," Dad replies. "Everyone will play better if we spend time warming up and doing drills at each practice."

I slump. "But what about batting? And stealing bases? And pitching strikes?"

Dad takes the plate of leftovers Mom left for him and pops it into the microwave. "We'll do plenty of throwing and hitting at our next practice," he says. "You'll get a chance to pitch too. And Annelise seems eager to pitch. She's got a good arm, that's for sure. And enough spunk to keep the batters on their toes!"

I cross my arms. "I've got spunk too," I grumble. "And I can throw the ball hard. You just have to give me my shot."

"I know you can throw hard!" he says. "I've seen you nail your sister with a pillow from all the way across the living room!" Dad glances around the kitchen. "Where is Sofia by the way? I haven't seen her for days."

I roll my eyes. Sometimes my dad can clown around as much as Henry. "You know she's at science camp, Dad. And I'm talking about pitching for games, not pillow fights."

"Pillow fight?" Lucas scampers into the kitchen, wearing his favorite robot pajamas, his hair still wet from his bath. He jumps into Dad's arms. "I love pillow fights! Can we have one, *por favor*?" he begs.

Dad turns Lucas upside down in his arms. "Sure!" he says. "We'll use you for the pillow!"

Lucas squeals with laughter as Dad gently bonks him against me. I can't help but smile too. My family likes to have fun together.

"Your sister and I were talking about softball games, not pillow fights," Dad tells Lucas as he sets him on his feet again.

Lucas jumps up and down like a grasshopper. "I like softball too!" he cries. "Can I be on Vicka's team?"

"Fine by me," I reply. "You can be our batboy."

"Yippee!" Lucas cries. "I'll be the best batboy ever! I even have a black cap and mask!"

I snort a laugh. "The batboy doesn't dress like a *bat*, Lucas," I tell my little brother. "He picks up the softball bats for the players after they hit the ball."

"Oh!" Lucas says. "I can do that!"

But Dad shakes his head. "You'll need to be a little bigger before you can take on that job, Lucas," he says.

Lucas slumps. "But I want to be on the team!"

The microwave starts beeping. Right on cue, Poco scampers into the kitchen and starts begging for a taste of Dad's supper. He dances around on his stubby hind legs, looking up at Dad with his big Chihuahua eyes.

"Tell you what, Lucas," Dad says, tossing Poco a bite of hamburger, "you can be our *dog* boy instead."

Lucas scrunches up his eyes. "*Dog* boy? What's that?" he asks.

"You'll be in charge of watching over our team mascot... Poco!" Dad replies, tossing our pup another morsel of food. Poco snatches it from the air faster than a catcher snatching the ball at home plate. *Chomp!*

Lucas brightens like a sunny day. "I can do that!" he exclaims. "Do I get to wear a dog costume?"

Dad shakes his head. "You'll wear a team shirt and hat, just like the rest of us!"

Lucas starts jumping up and down again. "Yes! I'm the dog boy!" He races out of the kitchen, Poco barking at his heels. "Mommy! Mommy!" he shouts. "Guess what? I'm going to be the team's dog boy!"

Dad chuckles as he carries his dinner to the dining room. I wander upstairs, Lucas's voice trailing after me as he tells Mom all about taking care of Poco at our games. Even my little brother thinks Dad's team is great. So far, I'm the only one who still isn't so sure.

Chapter 7

Give it a Whack, Cadillac!

When Bea and I get to our next practice, we start running around the ballpark, just like Dad told us to do if we arrive early. After listening to Lucas go on and on about helping the team, I gave myself a pep talk and ditched my foul attitude. I'm determined to show Dad I have what it takes to lead our team!

Bea is determined to lurk in the outfield. She's more interested in having fun and chatting in the dugout. I like doing that too, but I also really want to stand out. There's no better place to do that than standing on the pitcher's mound.

By the time we jog back to our practice field, other kids have arrived. Some of them are doing stretches. A few take off running around the ballpark. When Dad arrives a few minutes later, I'm surprised to see Uncle Julio is with him! Mom must be taking care of the music store today.

"*Hola*, Victoria!" Uncle Julio calls out as I run up to him and Dad.

"Hi, Uncle Julio!" I reply. "Did you come to watch me practice?"

"*¡Sí!*" Uncle Julio replies. "In fact, I came to *help* you practice."

My eyes go wide with surprise. "Really? What kind of help?"

Dad looks over from taking the equipment bags out of the van. He hands one to Uncle Julio, then grabs a stack of orange plastic cones. "After doing our warm-ups and drills, we'll divide the team into infield and outfield players," Dad explains. "Uncle Julio will work with the infielders on batting and base running. I'll work with the outfielders on catching and throwing."

I help Uncle Julio and Dad carry stuff to the ball diamond. "Were you as good a ball player as my dad was?" I ask my uncle.

"I hate to brag, but I've knocked a few out of the ballpark," Uncle Julio tells me, puffing up his chest with pride. He likes to clown around just as much as Dad. "Not as many as my bro, though. Your dad is the real champ in our family!"

Dad waves off Uncle Julio's compliment. "I haven't batted one out of the ballpark for twenty years. Besides, base hits are what win games. Everyone on the team is a champ when we all work together."

Uncle Julio leans in and whispers to me, "Still, it feels pretty good to slam one over the fence!"

I smile at my uncle. I don't plan to hit any home runs, but if I'm lucky, I'll strike out a batter or two!

Dad introduces Uncle Julio to everyone, then makes us do a bunch of stretches, ladder drills, and jump-roping. Finally, Dad says, "Let's spend some time warming up our arms. Did everyone bring a glove? Pair off, and we'll throw for a while."

We all grab our gloves and spread out. This time, I get paired with Annelise. Usually, I think of her as being more interested in tossing back her hair than tossing a ball around. Once, in phys ed, she chipped a nail while rebounding a basketball and made the coach let her sit out the rest of the game!

But something is different about her this summer. Each time she smacks the softball into my glove, I'm reminded of what Dad told me yesterday. Annelise has a good pitching arm and a lot of spunk. But so do I.

I can almost hear the umpire shouting, "Stee-rike!" as I imagine myself pitching strike after strike to the other team.

"Earth to Vicka," Annelise says. "Keep your head in the game!"

"Huh?" I say, looking up as Annelise points to the ball she just threw. It's lying in the grass by my feet.

"Oops," I say, picking it up. I glance across the field at Dad. *Did he see me miss that easy catch?* But thankfully he's busy giving Ed some pointers on fielding fly balls.

"Let's throw a few grounders now," Dad tells us a minute later.

We all start chucking the ball low so it bounces across the ground. To catch a grounder, we have to crouch down and hold our glove to the dirt. When the ball bounces in, we squeeze the glove closed like a trap to keep the ball from bouncing out again.

"Good nab, Vicka!" I hear someone call out as I snatch up the grounder Annelise just threw to me. I look over to see if it's Dad. But it's Drew! He throws me a smile, then chucks the ball to Henry.

"Thanks!" I call back to Drew, my heart morphing into a fluttery butterfly. I throw the ball to Annelise again, but I can't help glancing at Drew. The ball bounces way to the right of Annelise. She dives for it but misses.

"Stay focused," Annelise tells me as she stands up and brushes herself off. "If you're going to let a boy distract you during practice, what's going to happen when the other team shouts at you during a game?"

I try to brush aside Annelise's scolding, even though I know she's right. If I want to shine, I've got to keep my head in the game. But I can't help smiling to myself as I steal another look at Drew. Already my crush has noticed that I'm a good player! If I can keep it up, Dad is sure to notice me too.

After an hour of drills, Dad finally tells us to take a ten-minute break before we practice field positions. Annelise and I walk toward the dugout to get our water bottles. "Where do you hope to end up?" she asks me. "Infield or outfield?"

"Infield," I reply.

"Same here," Annelise replies. "I plan to be on the pitcher's mound."

I glance at Annelise. "Same here," I reply.

"I suppose I may need someone to relieve me once in a while," Annelise says.

Before I can say anything back, Bea and Julia jog over to us. "Come on, let's sit down for little bit," Bea says.

We take a seat on a shady patch of grass behind the dugout. We can see some of the other teams practicing on the other diamonds. Jenny's team is close by. Her mom is pitching balls as they take turns at bat. Jenny steps up to the plate. Her mom throws a pitch, and we hear the *ting!* of Jenny's bat striking the ball. Then we watch as the ball sails all the way out to center field. Her team whistles and cheers as Jenny runs the bases.

"Jenny's team is going to be hard to beat," Julia says as we watch the next batter step up to the plate. "Look at that guy! He's as big as a steamroller."

"I've seen him around," Bea says. "I think he's a year older than us."

"And a foot taller," Julia adds.

Steamroller chops at the ball so it skips across the dirt on its way to left field. The third-base player scoops up the ball so fast it's like he dipped his glove in superglue. He fires the ball to the pitcher. Steamroller chugs to a stop at first base.

"I hate to keep nagging, but when do we get to bat?" Julia asks again. Her expression is a mix of guilt and concern. "So far it's been mostly just running and throwing."

Bea and Julia look at me like I should know the answer. But it's Annelise who speaks up.

"We'll bat when Coach Torres says it's time to bat," she says matter-of-factly.

"My muscles hurt so much I'm not even sure I can lift a bat," Bea complains, rubbing her shoulder.

Julia nods. "My muscles are sore too." She flexes her bicep, then winces.

"No pain, no gain," Annelise says, stretching out her legs and reaching for her toes. "I was already in good shape because my mom and I work out all the time. And now that my dad has his own pool, I swim laps almost every day."

Just then Dad calls us all back together, saving us girls from another Annelise brag session.

"I forgot to mention earlier that I scheduled a scrimmage for next week against the Purple Poodles," Dad tells us.

"What's a scrimmage?" Min asks.

"It's a practice game," Dad replies. "It won't count for the season, but it will help both of our teams get ready to compete."

"Bowwow!" Henry barks. "We'll make puppy chow out of those poodles!"

Ed picks up a bat and gives it a hard swing. "Watch me hit one out of the ballpark!"

"Home runs are sweet, but getting runners on base is our goal. The more runners we have on base, the more runs we are likely to score," Dad tells Ed. "Make contact. That's the most important thing when you're at bat. I'd rather have you strike out than not swing the bat at all."

I shoot a look around at everyone. I thought the whole point of the game was hitting the ball as hard and as far as we can *without* getting a strike. Do the others think Dad is off base?

Dad turns to Uncle Julio. "Let's divide the group and get to work."

Uncle Julio nods and puts on a glove. "Who do I get to work with in the infield?"

I draw a lucky smiley face in the dirt with the toe of my cleat, hoping Dad will send me with Uncle Julio to practice pitching.

"I'll take Sam, Bea, and Vicka to the outfield," Dad says. The rest of the team will work on hitting and base running with you. Except for Annelise and Henry. They can go to the sidelines and work on pitching and catching for now."

Huh?

Everyone starts splitting up. I kick away the smiley face and stomp after Dad.

I can see Annelise throwing pitches to Henry from where I'm standing, way out in center field. The longer I watch them, the more my stomach churns.

Crack!

"Heads up, Vicka!" Dad shouts.

I look away from Annelise and see a pop fly sailing toward me. Without a moment to lose, I lift my glove and snatch it from the air, like Poco chomping a treat. Then I throw it back to Dad as hard as I can.

"*Bien hecho*, Victoria!" Dad shouts. "Excellent catch! Good throw!"

"Yeah, Vicka, good arm!" Sam adds.

Bea claps her hand against her glove for me.

But my friends' compliments wash over me like a bucket of ice water. I don't want to be good at catching and throwing. I want to be good at pitching. I can't do that if I'm stuck practicing in the outfield.

Finally, we switch places with the infielders. I wait for Uncle Julio to tell me to pitch some balls to Henry, but instead he calls Henry and Annelise over to bat with the rest of us.

"I'll pitch balls while you all take turns hitting," Uncle Julio says. "Swing at anything, okay? Even if it isn't in the strike zone."

Great, now Uncle Julio is starting to sound just like Dad!

"But . . . Uncle Julio," I blurt out. "If it's not a good pitch, we might strike out."

"That's why I want you to swing," he replies. "It's more important to take chances in softball than to play it safe." He looks around our group. "Swing at everything, got it? Keep your eye on the ball, and try to hit it."

Everyone lines up, waiting for a turn at bat. Uncle Julio stands in the pitcher's circle, a bucket of softballs by his side. Henry puts on a batting helmet and steps up to home plate.

"So, batter, are you ready?" Uncle Julio calls out to Henry.

Henry raises his bat. "Show me your stuff, Powder Puff," he razzes Uncle Julio.

Uncle Julio cracks a grin. "Let's see whatcha got, Hot Shot!" He winds up for the pitch. The ball snaps from his wrist and sails toward home plate. Henry grips the bat and steps into his swing.

CRACK!

The ball sails over Uncle Julio, past second base, and all the way to center field!

"Nice one!" Uncle Julio says, watching the ball land just inside the back fence. "A few more hits and we'll be calling you Home Run Henry!"

Henry grins from ear to ear. Then he gets ready to hit again. This time, Uncle Julio throws a curveball. Henry swings, but the ball slips past his bat and hits the backstop instead.

Thunk!

"Shoot," Henry says. "Strike one."

"But you swung like you meant it!" Uncle Julio says. He looks at the rest of us. "When you step up to the plate, *own* it. Show the other team who's boss."

Henry raises his bat again and leans in. "*I'm* the boss, Applesauce!" he shouts.

This time Uncle Julio pitches the ball so low that Henry has to swing his bat like a golf club.

Ting!

The ball pops up high. Uncle Julio runs forward to catch it, but stumbles and falls to the dirt.

"*¡Ay!*" Uncle Julio brushes himself off as he stands up again, laughing. "Way to make me eat dirt, Henry!"

"Anytime, Coach," Henry replies.

"Batter up!" Uncle Julio calls out.

Bea gives me a nudge. "Your turn, Vicka!"

I try to take confident strides as I walk toward the plate, even though my legs feel as stiff as baseball bats. Henry hands me his bat and helmet. "Give it a whack, Cadillac."

I give Henry a firm nod, then put on the helmet.

Uncle Julio tosses me a grin as I take my place in the batter's box. I cringe, hoping he doesn't say something embarrassing like, "Is that my little niece I see?" But if he does, I can't let it bother me. Like Annelise said, I have to stay focused if I want to be a winner.

But Uncle Julio doesn't say a word as I raise my bat and bend my knees. A moment later, I'm swinging with all my might at the bright yellow blur that's zooming toward me.

Ting!

The ball sails toward first base! It lands foul, but still, I hit it! Hard!

"Atta girl, Vicka!" Uncle Julio calls out. "Choke up on the bat a little. Let's see if that will keep the ball in play."

I move my hands up a notch on the bat. This time when I hit the ball it sails right between first and second base! I can hear Bea and the others cheering for me.

I strike out on my third try, but I'm so excited about my two solid hits, I feel like prancing around like Poco. I'm bursting with pride as I walk back to the others and feel them pat me on the back, complimenting me on my good swing.

Even Annelise looks impressed. "Not bad, Vicka," she tells me. "With a little more practice, you could be as good as *me*."

On the way home after practice, I tell Dad about my two good hits.

"I heard!" Dad says. "Uncle Julio filled me in. He said you have a strong swing and that you're not afraid of the ball."

I beam with pride. It almost makes up for having to watch Annelise practice pitching when I was stuck in the outfield.

"So when will I get to practice pitching, Dad?" I ask.

"You'll get your chance," Dad replies. "From what I saw today, we're shaping up to be a pretty good team! With a little more practice, we'll be ready to give the Purple Poodles a run for their money at our scrimmage next week!"

Chapter 8

Poco Saves the Day. Not.

Dad was right. By the end of the week, we really are starting to play like a team! Henry is our catcher. He can handle the ball well and is big enough to make any third-base runner think twice about sliding into him at home plate. Plus, unlike the rest of us, he doesn't mind eating dirt.

"Puts hair on my chest!" Henry brags every time he spits out dust with his sunflower seed shells.

Julia is the tallest player on our team. She can reach the farthest to catch a ball or tag out a runner without taking her foot off the base, so Dad wants her to play first base. Ed is a pro at guarding second base. He's our cutter too. That means he helps the outfielders get the ball back to the infield as fast as possible so we can make an out or keep a runner on base. Min is playing shortstop, Drew is on third, Bea is in left field, happily jamming to her music, and Sam owns right field. Tara and Tony play different positions, depending on who needs a break.

Dad kept his word and has been letting me practice pitching with Annelise. I hate to admit it, but she is a really good pitcher. But *my* pitch is rock solid too! Hopefully, Dad realizes it and let's me be the starting pitcher for today's scrimmage against the Poodles.

Other teams are scrimmaging today too, so the ballpark is buzzing with people. Uncle Julio has been giving me lots of good tips between practices, and Jenny has been coming over to catch for me in my backyard while Bea entertains us with her playlist. With some pitching practice against the Poodles, I'm sure to outshine Annelise by the time we play our first real game.

Our team shirts and hats just arrived, so we all scramble to put them on for the scrimmage. They are bubblegum pink with a Chihuahua printed on the front. Even though the Chihuahua is snarling, it still looks sweet, just like Poco.

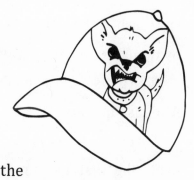

Annelise struts up and down the third-base line in her team shirt and cap, waving to everyone like she's walking on a pageant runway. Even though this is only a scrimmage, lots of Chihuahua and Poodle fans are here to watch us play, including Mom and Abuela! Lucas is here too, walking Poco on a leash, letting people pet him as he wags his tail. Lucas and Poco look übercute in their matching pink team tees!

The guys are sitting inside the dugout, trying to spit sunflower seed shells through the wire mesh, aiming for Annelise. Henry takes careful aim, then spits a shell that sticks to Annelise's arm as she walks by doing her queenly wave!

The guys practically fall off the bench, laughing, as Annelise howls.

"Gross!" she says wiping the slimy shell off her arm. She marches up to the dugout, snarling just like the Chihuahua on her shirt. "Were you born in a barn?" she barks at the boys.

"Moo," Henry says, then spits another shell. This one lands on Annelise's pink cleat! She kicks at the dust like a donkey until the shell falls off.

"This is it team!" Dad says, gathering us together in the dugout before the scrimmage is set to begin. "Today we test our determination to have fun and play well! The Poodles are short a player today. Would one of you volunteer to play for them? It's just a scrimmage, so all we're trying to do is get a little game practice in before the real season begins next week."

"I'll do it, Coach," Julia says, raising her hand.

"Great! Thank you, Julia," Dad replies as he makes a note on his clipboard. "That means Tara will play first base, and Tony will be on the bench, for now. I'll work you into the lineup later, Tony."

Tony nods and leans back on the dugout bench. "I'll hold down the fort," he says, propping his hands behind his head.

"Here's the batting order," Dad continues. "Bea, Min, and Ed will lead off. Drew, I want you to bat cleanup."

"*Cleanup?*" Annelise says, giving Drew the once over. "He's been wearing the same dirty socks to practice all week."

Drew grins, then spits a shell.

"So what?" Henry puts in. "I've been wearing the same dirty socks all summer!" He leans down and pulls up his droopy socks. Then he reties the tangled laces on his dusty cleats.

Annelise gives him the stink eye.

"What does cleanup mean?" Bea asks.

"It means Drew is one of our best hitters," Sam says. "If you, Min, and Ed can get on base, our chances are good Drew will hit at least one of you home."

Drew ducks his eyes, but I can see his ears pink up with pride over Dad's choice of making him our cleanup hitter.

Dad finishes with the batting order, then looks at Annelise. "How is your pitching arm today?" he asks her.

Annelise makes a muscle. "Perfect, as usual!" she replies.

Dad nods. "Let's see how you pitch against the Poodles, then."

"You can count on me, Coach," Annelise says. "I'll make those poodles *beg* for mercy."

I look bug-eyed at Dad as everyone else groans at Annelise's joke. "I'm not pitching for the scrimmage?" I ask him.

"I want you in center field, Vicka," Dad replies. "I'm counting on that good arm of yours to catch fly balls and throw them all the way to the infield!" He looks at the others and continues. "The Poodles are batting first, so grab your gloves and get out on the diamond. Thanks again, Julia, for volunteering to play for the other team."

"No problem, Coach," Julia says, jogging out of our dugout and over to the Poodles'. Everyone else starts heading out too. I just sit there, weighed down by Dad's decision to send me to center field.

A minute later, Tony gives me a nudge. "Better get going, Vicka," he tells me. "Or do you want me to play for you?"

"No," I say. "I just . . . I have to catch my breath."

"Whatever," Tony says, standing up and stretching. "I'm gonna refill my water bottle. All these salty sunflower seeds are making me thirsty."

As Tony leaves the dugout, I take off my glasses and rub the sting from my eyes. I really wanted to pitch today. I can't believe that Dad chose Annelise instead.

A bag of sunflower seeds is lying next to me on the bench. One of the boys must have left it there. Instead of putting my glasses on again, I hide them under the bag of seeds. Then I stand up and pretend to look around for something I lost.

"Oh, no!" I say loudly, as I glance all around the dugout. "Where can they be?"

"Did you lose something, Vicka?" someone asks.

I look through the dugout doorway and see Lucas giving Poco a bowl of water.

"Um . . . my glasses," I say, feeling my stomach tighten. I don't like telling fibs, especially not to my family. But this is an emergency. I can't shine if I'm stuck way out in center field. And I can't see well enough to catch a fly ball without my glasses. But I *can* see home plate from the pitcher's mound without them. Maybe Dad will put Annelise in the outfield and let me pitch instead. It's a long-shot plan, but, unfortunately, it's the only one I've got at the moment.

Lucas hooks Poco's leash to the dugout bench. "I'll help you look for your glasses, Vicka!" he says.

"No!" I snap. "I mean . . . there's no need for that, Lucas. I must have left them at home. You take care of Poco. I'll go tell Dad."

I hurry out of the dugout before Lucas can ask any more questions. Dad is standing in the pitcher's circle with Annelise and Henry, going over the signals they'll use for the scrimmage. When Dad touches the brim of his hat or his shoulder or rubs his nose it means different things, like walk the batter or be ready for a steal or throw a strike.

The three of them look up as I put on the brakes. "What is it, Vicka?" Dad asks. "You look worried. Is something wrong?"

I nod. "Um . . . I can't find my glasses. I must have left them at home."

Annelise frowns. "You had them on earlier."

"Um . . . no . . . those were just my sunglasses," I say, thinking fast. "I need my *real* glasses to see the ball from a long way away." Turning to Dad I say, "If you put me in center field, I'll miss a lot of catches. But if you let me pitch, then everything will be fine because —"

"Vicka! I found them!" someone shouts.

We all look toward the dugout. Lucas takes Poco by the leash and runs toward us, his face beaming with pride. A pair of glasses are in his hand.

My glasses.

¡Uf!

"They were in the dugout!" Lucas says as he hurries up to us. "You must have set them down and someone put a bag of sunflower seeds on top of them!" He holds my glasses out to me.

My shoulders sag. *"Gracias,"* I mumble even though I'm not feeling very thankful. I take the glasses from my brother and put them on.

"You should thank Poco too," Lucas says. "He knocked the sunflower seeds off the bench when he was sniffing around. That's when I saw your glasses."

Dad pats Poco's head. "*Gracias*, Poco! You saved the day."

"Yip-yip!" Poco wags his tail.

"Problem solved," Annelise says. "Now will everyone please leave so I can warm up?"

"As you wish, your highness!" Henry bows like a servant before his queen, reties his loose laces again, then heads to home plate.

Dad takes Lucas and Poco back to the dugout.

I trudge to center field.

Bea waves to me from left field. Sam tips his hat to me from right.

I stand squarely in the middle, glaring sharply at Annelise from under the brim of my pink softball cap. But I'm so far away from the infield, she probably can't see my squinty eyes. Besides, her back is turned to me as she practices throwing the ball to Henry from the pitcher's mound. *My* pitcher's mound.

Secretly, I make a few *un*lucky wishes. "Let her pitch waddle like a duck," I mumble to myself. "Make her throw the ball to first base instead of getting a runner out on third . . ."

But instead of making me feel better, my wishes make me feel lower than the toe of Henry's dirty sweat sock. It would have been easier to wish bad things on Annelise earlier this year because she was such a bully to everyone. But she hasn't been nearly as bossy during softball. In fact, she's been acting like a better sport than me. Is she meant to rule the diamond? Maybe softball is her way to shine, not mine.

"Hey, Vicka! Heads up!" I look toward right field. Sam gets ready to throw the ball to me as we warm up for the game. It's an easy catch, but I let the ball hit the ground instead. When I throw it to Bea, I don't use all my strength so it dribbles across the grass to her feet.

I turn to see if Dad is watching me. But he's talking with the Poodles' coach. When I look toward the stands, my heart sinks. Mom and Abuela are waving to me. They're always telling Sofia, Lucas, and me to make the best of every situation. But if I play my best today, Dad will probably keep me out here in the middle of nowhere for the rest of the season. If I play poorly in the outfield, maybe he'll realize his mistake and put me on the pitcher's mound where I belong.

I give Mom and Abuela a weak wave, then glance away. My eyes land on Drew. He's warming up his arm at third, throwing the ball around the bases. If I can convince Dad I belong on the mound, my crush will see me sparkle at the center of the diamond.

"Play ball!" the umpire shouts.

This is it. Decision made. I have to prove to Dad I don't belong way out here. I am about to play the worst game of my unfortunately average life.

The first Poodle steps up to the plate. Annelise pitches the ball.

Ting!

The ball sails in a high arch over second base. It's coming all the way to center field. "Catch it, Vicka!" I hear Drew shout from third base.

¡Uf! My crush is watching me! But I know Dad is watching too. I pretend the sun is in my eyes and let the ball thump to the grass.

"Throw it in!" Ed calls to me from second base.

I look up and see the runner rounding first. I pick up the ball and throw it wild. It sails past Ed and skips across the infield dirt. Annelise snatches it up and dashes back to her position. The runner is safe on second base.

On the pitching mound, Annelise locks eyes with me. By the look on her face, I can tell she's wondering how I could miss such an easy catch and then make such a sloppy throw. I duck my eyes and count the dandelions at my feet.

"Good try, Vicka!" Bea shouts from left field.

"You'll get it next time!" Sam shouts from right field.

As the next batter steps to the plate, I look across the diamond and see Dad watching me. "Come on, Vicka!" he shouts. "Stay focused!"

I duck my eyes again. Now, I feel lower than the lowest toe on the dirtiest sock in all of Middleton.

"Right in the pocket, pitcher!" Henry shouts to Annelise as he hunkers down behind the plate. But she pitches the ball outside of the strike zone. She walks the batter. She walks the next one too.

Why doesn't Dad tell her *to stay focused?* I think. If I were pitching, we would have three batters out right now! Instead, the bases are loaded.

Julia, from our team, steps up to the plate to bat for the Poodles.

Annelise looks nervous as she winds up for the pitch and throws the ball hard. This time it's heading right for Julia!

Quickly, Julia tries to turn out of the way, but the ball hits her in the back with a hollow *thump!*

"Ouchies!" Bea says from left field. "Poor Julia!"

Julia steps out of the batter's box, wincing in pain. She crouches down and wraps her arms around herself, trying not to cry. She cries anyway.

The ump calls for a time out as Henry pulls off his catcher's mask and kneels beside Julia, patting her shoulder.

Julia rubs the tears from her cheeks as Dad walks over to check on her. Dad asks her something, and I see Julia shake her head. I wonder if she's going to need someone else to run the bases for her.

Finally I see Henry put on his mask again and straighten his chest pad. Julia takes a deep breath and shakes out her arms a bit. She gives Dad a small smile.

Dad nods, then looks at the umpire.

The ump shouts, "Batter, take your base!" I'm so relieved. Julia is one tough cookie to keep playing.

She jogs to first base. The runner on third base jogs home to score a run for the Poodles. The score is Poodles 1, Chihuahuas 0.

"Um . . . sorry about that," Annelise calls to Julia from the mound.

Julia gives her a nod. "It's okay, Annelise. It was an accident."

"C'mon, pitcher!" Henry calls, squatting down and punching the pocket of his catcher's mitt. "Right down the middle this time."

Annelise takes a deep breath as the next batter steps up to the plate. Despite my bad wishes, Annelise zeros in, winds up for the pitch, then lets the ball fly from her fingertips. This time it zooms straight for the zone.

The batter swings.

Ting!

The ball flies over Annelise's outstretched glove and sails on to center field.

If I catch it, I will shine — but not as the pitcher.

I fake a stumble, then watch the ball thump to the ground. Two more Poodles score, and Julia is rounding third base. I look up to see if Dad is running over to check on me and tell me I obviously don't belong in the outfield. But he isn't running toward me. He's frowning at me — big time. Like he knows a fake stumble when he sees one.

Ed snatches up the ball and throws it as hard as he can to Henry. Henry plants himself in front of the plate, ready to make the catch and tag Julia out. But Julia slides, knocking Henry off his feet and the ball from his mitt.

"Safe!" the ump shouts.

All the Poodles cheer.

Henry is slow to get up, like he just got trampled by a herd of poodles. He pulls off his mask and limps around in a circle, rubbing his leg.

"Keep it together, Hen!" Drew calls from third base. "There's no crying in softball!" Drew grins playfully.

"I ain't crying," Henry grumps, rubbing his leg. "Just got some dirt in my eyes, that's all."

Julia brushes dust off her uniform and smiles as she chalks up another run for the Poodles.

Chapter 9

Ice Cream Conversations

Even though Henry hit a home run for our team in the last inning of our scrimmage, the Poodles still beat us, 4-1. And even though I kept blowing plays, Dad didn't put me on the mound. Instead, he put me on the bench and let Tony play center field.

After we line up to shake hands with the Poodles, everyone takes off for Java Jane's. Win or lose, Dad promised to treat the Chihuahuas to ice cream after the game.

But just as I'm about to hop on my bike and head out with Bea and the others, I hear Dad say, "Hang on, Vicka. I want to talk with you for a minute."

I feel like Poco with his tail between his legs after he chews up a couch pillow or overturns one of Mom's potted plants on our porch. No one blamed me for losing the scrimmage, but I know it was mostly my fault. I could have played to win, but I didn't.

After everyone leaves, I meet Dad by his van. "What was going on out there today?" he asks me. "I know you can play better than that, Victoria. I don't expect you to make every play, but I do expect you to try."

"I *was* trying!" I fire back.

"Trying to *lose*, if you ask me," Dad says.

I cross my arms over my chest. "It's just . . . I'm a crummy outfielder," I say. "You should have let me pitch! I'm just as good as Annelise!"

"Is that what this is about?" Dad shakes his head. "I expect Lucas to throw a tantrum when he doesn't get his way, not you."

Angry tears spring to my eyes. "I wasn't throwing a tantrum! I played the best I could!"

"No, you didn't," Dad snaps. "Not by a long shot." He picks up an equipment bag and throws it into the back of the van, closing the hatch. *Thunk!*

Tears gush from my eyes as I storm away from Dad. Sobbing, I fumble with my bike, climb on, and pedal as hard as I can out of the ballpark.

Drew was wrong.

There *is* crying in softball.

I take the long way to Java Jane's so I can calm down. By the time I get there I've stopped crying, but my throat still aches with tears. I swallow them down, paste on a cheerful smile, and walk inside. The place is packed with softball players. I guess Dad isn't the only coach who likes to treat his team to ice cream.

The coffee shop door opens again. I turn to see Dad walk in. When he sees me, he freezes. "Vicka, I —" he starts to say.

But I turn away and push through the crowd to where my team is sitting.

When Drew sees Dad he shouts, "Heads up, Chihuahuas! Coach is here!"

Everyone turns and looks. The boys start yipping like Chihuahuas. The girls join in. We didn't win the scrimmage, but Dad gives them high fives all around. "First, we celebrate playing a good, solid game," he tells us. When he catches my eye, I look away. "Then, we'll go over the stats and see what we need to work on for next time."

I pull up a chair next to Bea while Dad takes ice cream orders from everyone — chocolate, vanilla, or twist cones. When he gets to me I say, "No, thank you. I'm not hungry," without even looking up.

Bea looks up from her phone. "I am! Chocolate, please!" she tells Dad. Then she turns to me. "I just texted Jenny to ask how her scrimmage went with the Dalmatians. Look at her reply!" She holds up her phone for me.

We beat the spots off them!!

"Good for her," I say halfheartedly. I'm happy for Jenny, but I'm still upset about my fight with Dad.

Bea gives me a worried look. "Is everything okay? Your eyes look red and puffy."

"Allergies," I reply.

Bea nods. "What took you so long to get here?" she asks. "I would have waited longer, but Annelise dragged me along as a shield against the boys. They were spitting sunflower seed shells at us the whole way here!" Bea ruffles her hair, and a sunflower shell falls out.

"My dad wanted me to . . . um . . . help him with the equipment," I tell Bea. "It took longer than we thought, that's all."

Bea looks relieved. "Oh, good. I'm glad nothing is wrong. Next time, ask me to help!"

Just then the coffee shop door bursts open, and a bunch of softball players wearing blue caps and shirts pile in, whooping and hollering, "We're number one! We're number one!" The last player through the door is Jenny! Her mom is right behind her.

Dad walks over to talk with Jenny's mom while everyone starts digging into the ice cream. Even though I said I wasn't hungry, Dad got a vanilla cone for me anyway. I eat it, but I barely taste it.

Jenny smiles from ear to ear when she sees Bea and me. She hurries up to us. "Did you get my text?" she asks. "We won our scrimmage!"

"Yes!" Bea and I say, giving Jenny high fives.

"Did you guys win too?" Jenny asks, squeezing in next to me on my chair.

I don't answer.

"Nope," Bea says. "We lost, four to one."

"Bummer!" Jenny says.

"Soon we'll be beating *you* and the rest of your scruffy pack." We all look up and see Annelise standing over us, licking a chocolate cone, and squinting at Jenny.

Jenny's jaw tightens when she sees Annelise. Then she relaxes into a thin smile. "Maybe so," she replies, "but we'll make you work for it."

Annelise makes a face like she's eating sour grapes instead of ice cream. "Shouldn't you get back to your *friends*?" she asks Jenny, glancing at the other Huskies sitting across the coffee shop. "This is a private party for our team." She takes another lick from her cone.

Jenny rolls her eyes and turns away from Annelise. "Let's hang out later, okay?" she says to Bea and me. "We could bat some balls around for practice."

Now Bea makes a sour-grapes face. "I've had enough softball for one day. Julia, Min, and I are going to the pool."

"Okay, I'm in!" Jenny says.

"I'll go too," I say. I don't feel like swimming, but sitting by the pool will be better than going home with Dad.

"Next time, ask me to invite you to my dad's house to swim," Annelise says to us as Jenny ducks back to her team. "We don't need the *Jen*-emy hanging around. "

As everyone finishes their ice cream and starts taking off from Java Jane's, I tell Bea I'll catch up to her and the other girls, then I text Mom to tell her I'm going to the pool. When Dad is ordering himself a cup of coffee to go, I slip out before I have to talk to him.

But when I get outside, I feel a tap on my shoulder. Turning around, I see Annelise shaking her head at me.

"Now what?" I ask. "If you're upset with me for not treating Jenny like a frenemy, you're wasting your time. She's my friend, and I'm not —"

"That's not it," Annelise cuts in. "I didn't want to say anything in front of the others, but I know you messed up on purpose today. Don't look so shocked. You know it's true. I've seen you catch and throw. You're as good as me. Why did you try to lose?"

"I wasn't trying to lose," I say. "I was trying to show my dad I don't belong in the outfield. But it didn't work. Congratulations. It looks like you are the team's top-dog pitcher."

I wait for a smug smile to spread across Annelise's face. It's got to be her dream come true to be the coach's number-one pick. Instead, she looks like I just socked her in the stomach.

"I thought we were *friends*," she says. "But friends don't quit on each other. They challenge each other to do their *best*." She crosses her arms and locks eyes with me. "Your dad is a good coach. Like it or not, putting you in center field is a smart strategy. You're better at fielding fly balls than I am. With you in center field and Ed cutting for us, we can keep the runs to a minimum. That's called teamwork."

Annelise climbs up onto her bike. "If you want to be the star, then pick a solo sport like bungee jumping or running marathons. In softball, we need each other."

As Annelise bikes away, I think about how there was a time when I wouldn't have given her advice a second thought. In elementary school, I avoided her like the plague. It was the only way to keep from getting teased or pushed around on the playground. But middle school has thrown us together, again and again. Not always in a good way, but not always in a bad way either. Is it smart to take advice from someone who used to be my number-one enemy? Is it even possible to be friends with someone like that?

As much as I hate to admit it, somewhere in her gritty opinions there is a glimmer of truth.

I could keep flubbing up in center field. It will get me lots of attention, but it's not the kind of attention I want. I want my teammates to notice me for doing my best and making our team the best that it can be. And I want Dad to feel proud of me, not disappointed because I have to get my way or I'll throw a tantrum.

Even though Annelise is an expert at putting other people down when they stand in her way, she's a better sport than me these days. Now it's my turn to step up to the plate and be the best center fielder I can be. After all, who better to play in the middle of the field than the most average girl around?

Chapter 10

Lucky Charms

"Guys, I figured out what we need to win games!" Henry tells us at practice a couple weeks later. So far, we've lost against the Poodles, the Dalmatians, and the Pugs.

Annelise and I look over from throwing pitches to each other. Ever since our talk at Java Jane's, we've been practicing together. Sometimes Jenny practices with us too, even though Annelise ices her out the whole time. She still thinks we should treat Jenny, Katie, and Grace like frenemies since they are Huskies.

"What do we need?" Min asks Henry, looking up from her stretching. "A miracle?"

"Nope," Henry says. "All we need is luck."

"I could have told you that," Ed adds, spitting a sunflower seed.

"What I mean is, we need a lucky *charm*," Henry explains.

"Like the breakfast cereal?" Sam asks, balancing a bat on the palm of his hand like a circus performer. "I love that stuff. I always eat the marshmallows and leave the cereal for my brother." He chuckles. "You should hear him holler when he pours a bowlful."

Henry shakes his head. "I'm not talking about cereal," he says. "I'm talking about doing stuff that will bring our team good luck before each game!"

"You mean like, carry a four-leaf clover around?" I ask. "Or use a lucky bat?"

"Exactly!" Henry replies. "Remember when I made that awesome home run at our scrimmage against the Poodles?"

We all nod.

"It was legendary," Drew adds, "even though we still lost. But what's that got to do with —"

"Let me explain," Henry says, cutting in. "The morning of the scrimmage, I put new laces in my cleats. But they kept coming untied, so right before it was my turn at bat, I triple-knotted them. Poco was sniffing around in the dugout doorway, so I hopped over him on my way to grab a bat. Next thing I knew, I was smashing a ball over the fence!"

Henry looks at our blank faces, like all of this is supposed to make sense. "Triple-knots and hops . . ." he says. "That's what we need to win!"

Annelise rolls her eyes. "That's the dumbest thing I have ever heard. Next, you'll be telling us not to wash our socks because that will bring us good luck too."

Henry brightens even more. "I almost forgot! I was wearing dirty socks that day! Good call, Annelise. Add it to the lucky-charms list!"

Tony looks over from jumping rope. "Are you saying all we have to do is tie some knots in our laces and hop to the batter's box, and we'll start winning?" he asks.

Henry nods. "Plus, wear dirty socks. That's it! We'll be champs!"

Annelise groans.

Tony nods, then starts jumping again. "Makes sense to me."

Henry grins.

Bea shrugs. "It can't hurt to try. Remember what Coach Torres told us? We have to think like a team. If we all have the same good-luck charms, it will bond us together, and that will make us play better."

"Plus, when the other teams see us hopping up and down like bunny rabbits," Ed adds, "they'll be too busy rolling around on the ground laughing at us to get us out on base."

Annelise snorts. "They'll think we're freaks," she says, rolling her eyes.

"I don't mind being a freak if it means we'll win some games," Tara says.

Annelise crosses her arms. "I absolutely refuse to wear dirty socks."

"Then prepare for bad luck, Annelise," Henry says, rubbing extra dirt on his socks.

As Dad calls us out to practice, Henry reties his cleats into triple knots, then hops through the dugout doorway. Soon everyone is rubbing dirt on their socks, triple-knotting their laces, and hopping onto the diamond too.

"You're all nuttier than a candy bar if you believe Henry," Annelise sasses as we all hop past her. "Good luck . . . bad luck . . . there's no such thing."

But as I glance back into the dugout a moment later, I see Annelise bend over and triple-knot her laces. She doesn't rub dirt on her socks, but she does take a tiny hop on her way out of the dugout door.

Maybe there's some truth to Henry's good-luck charms, because we win our next two games! By the time the softball season is half over, the Pink Chihuahuas scoring record is two wins and two losses, not counting the scrimmage.

Everyone is super happy about our wins, but I can't stop feeling like a loser. Dad has kept quiet about our argument after the scrimmage. I haven't brought it up either. Even though we act like everything is normal, it feels like there is a big hole between us now. The kind Poco sometimes digs in our backyard. But this hole keeps getting bigger and bigger all by itself. If I get too close to the edge of it, I might fall in. So I keep my distance from Dad.

Today we're playing the Blue Huskies. They are undefeated! If we could beat them and break their winning streak, it would be the ultimate way to shine.

I get to the field extra early before our game, so I can take a run around the ballpark to loosen up. Dad was right. Running is really getting me in good shape. All of us are playing better now than we did at the start of the season. We're not the greatest team in the league, but we're not the worst team either. The Chihuahuas are somewhere in the middle, just like me.

As I jog along, I think about the other things Dad has been right about lately. Like making us jump rope and do ladder drills and swing at every pitch during practice. At first all those drills seemed lame. But now I understand why he made us do them.

Maybe he was right to put me in center field too, I think. *I do have a strong arm and a good throw. And, like Annelise said, softball isn't a solo sport. It takes everyone working together to make plays and win games.*

As I round the last corner and head back to where I started, Dad's van pulls into the ballpark. I stop and watch as he gets out. He walks to the back of the van, opens the hatch, and starts taking out the equipment bags.

It feels like I'm standing on the edge of that big, deep hole again. If I take a step, I might fall in. But if I don't, it will just keep getting bigger. I take a deep breath, and walk over to Dad. "Can I help?" I ask, reaching for one of the bags.

Dad looks up, surprised. Then a smile breaks across his face. "Sure thing, Bonita!" He slides one of the bags toward me. But I don't pick it up right away.

I fiddle with the zipper on the bag. "I just wanted to say . . . I'm sorry . . . for fighting with you," I say quietly. "And for getting so upset about playing in the outfield. I wanted to be the star of the team. Instead, I let the team down. I let *you* down. I'm really sorry."

Dad is quiet for a minute. Then he puts his arm around my shoulders. "I'm sorry too," he tells me, kissing the top of my head. "Maybe it was a bad idea for me to coach your team. Looking back, I should have checked with you first or volunteered to coach a different team."

"I-it's okay, Dad," I say, sniffling back my tears. "Y-you're a good coach. Everyone says so, even Annelise, and she only says nice things about people once in a million years."

Dad laughs a little. "From now on, let's talk things out instead of fighting . . . deal?"

"Deal," I reply.

Dad hugs me tight.

I hug him tighter.

When Bea and Jenny arrive a few minutes later, we crank Bea's music, sing along with the lyrics, and play air guitar in the outfield. Suddenly I realize this is exactly how I wanted to spend my summer — having fun with my best friends!

As everyone else arrives, Jenny takes off to warm up with her teammates. "Good luck!" she calls over her shoulder to Bea and me.

"You'll need it!" Bea calls back in a teasing voice.

After we all warm up with some running and stretching, Dad has Annelise practice pitches with

Henry. That same old twinge of jealousy zips through me at first, but I don't let it eat me up like I did earlier in the season. Instead, I take up my position, smack dab in the middle of center field.

The grass is still damp with morning dew. The sunshine is making the outfield look bright and sparkly. Even the dandelions look brighter today. Or maybe it's me, Victoria Torres, that's making everything shine. The stands are filling up with Chihuahua and Husky fans. More than anything, I want to show them my team is determined to play our best. Bending over a little, hands on my knees, I'm ready for anything.

After throwing the ball around the field, Dad gathers us together in our dugout for a final pep talk before the game begins. Annelise winces and rubs her shoulder as she sits down next to me on the bench.

"Are you okay?" I ask her.

"I think I pulled a muscle while I was warming up," she tells me. "And look at this . . ." She holds up her

hand and wiggles her pointer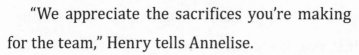
finger. "I chipped a nail!"

Everyone looks over at
the small chip on Annelise's pink
polished nail.

"We appreciate the sacrifices you're making
for the team," Henry tells Annelise.

But instead of saying something sassy back to
Henry, Annelise looks at Dad. "I should really ice my
shoulder, Coach. Maybe Vicka could pitch the first
inning against the Huskies? Obviously, her nails
aren't in danger of chipping."

I hide my plain, slightly chewed nails in my lap
and blink with surprise at Annelise. Did she just offer
to step down from her diamond throne to let me pitch
in her place? Maybe she has something up her sleeve,
but it doesn't seem like it. In fact, she looks super
sincere. Like she really wants to give me a chance
to shine on the pitcher's mound during our biggest
game of the season.

Everyone is quiet, waiting for Dad's decision.

He thinks for a moment then says, "That's not a bad idea, Annelise. Aside from giving your arm a rest, the Husky's coach was watching you warm up your pitches just now. She was even jotting notes on her clipboard. She's probably coaching her team to bat against *you*. If we put a new pitcher on the mound, it will throw the Huskies a curveball right from the start."

"Ooo . . . that's sneaky," Min says.

"It's not sneaky," Drew puts in. "It's strategy."

Henry nods. "Sneaky strategy . . . I like it!" He looks at me. "C'mon, Vicka. You've got to pitch for us."

Everyone murmurs in agreement. Bea reaches over and squeezes my arm. "You can do it, Bestie!"

I bite my lip nervously and look at Dad. "Are you sure?" I ask.

Dad smiles. "Positive, Bonita."

I smile back. "Okay, Coach, I'll try," I say. But as everyone gives me high fives, I feel my pitching arm turn to jelly. At the start of the season, I wanted to pitch more than anything. Now that I have the chance, I wonder if I've got what it takes to beat the best team in the league.

After I warm up with a few pitches to Henry, the Huskies send their first batter to the plate. It's Grace!

"Play ball!" the umpire shouts.

"Show her who's boss, Applesauce," Henry calls to me.

I pitch the ball as hard as I can. Unfortunately, Grace whacks it for a base hit. Sam fields the ball and throws it back to me.

As I get ready to pitch again, Grace leads off like she's itching to steal second base. Quickly, I turn to throw the ball to Julia on first, hoping we can get Grace out. But it's not a good throw, and Julia bobbles the ball. She scrambles to pick it up.

"She's going!" Henry shouts as Grace takes off for second base. Ed makes like he wants Julia to throw the ball, but Dad shouts, "Hold it!"

In a panic, Julia throws the ball anyway. Ed reaches for it, but the ball flies past his glove. Grace barely touches second base before taking off for third.

Bea grabs the ball from the grass and throws it as hard as she can to me. Fortunately, I make the catch and hurry back to the pitcher's circle with the ball. Grace is safe on third. I'm red faced on the pitcher's mound. We all messed up on that play.

"Brush it off, Chihuahuas!" Dad calls to us. Then he looks at me. "Focus, Vicka. You can do this."

I take a deep breath as the next Husky steps up to the plate.

"Here we go, pitcher!" Henry shouts.

I throw my best pitch.

Crack!

"Bea!" I shout as the ball sails toward left field. "Heads up!"

But Bea has gone back to singing along with one of her softball songs, kicking up dandelion seeds. "Huh?" she says, as the ball crash-lands a few feet in front of her.

The batter is on his way to first, and Grace is running full steam ahead, for home!

Bea manages to get the ball to Ed, who chucks it hard to Henry. Grace starts her slide just as Henry catches the ball. But when he reaches down to tag Grace, he touches her shoulder, not her foot, which is already slamming into home plate.

"Safe!" the umpire shouts.

Cheers erupt from the stands. Blue Husky fans are on their feet, clapping and whistling for their team. Two pitches, and the Huskies are on the scoreboard. *¡Uf!* Maybe it was a mistake to let me pitch?

"You've got this, Vicka!" I hear Annelise yell from the dugout.

I try to soak up Annelise's confidence before throwing my next pitch. Somehow, I manage to strike out the next batter. Then Min catches a pop fly, and Drew makes an out on third. We all trudge to the dugout, Huskies 1, Chihuahuas 0.

"No wonder we're behind," Henry says, pointing to Annelise's ankles. "You're wearing clean socks!"

Annelise rolls her eyes and adjusts the ice pack on her shoulder. "We're behind because of our errors, not because of my socks."

"How is your shoulder feeling?" I ask her, halfway hoping she feels good enough to pitch.

Annelise rotates her arm. "It's still a little stiff. You better plan on pitching the next inning too."

Unfortunately, Min and Ed both strike out at bat. But Drew, our cleanup hitter, bats the ball straight to first base. He gets out, but Bea gets to third. Then she scores.

"Way to take one for the team," Henry says, patting Drew on the back when it's our turn to take the field again. The game is tied 1-1 at the top of the second inning.

Dad puts me back on the pitcher's mound. Somehow we manage to keep the Huskies from scoring, even though my arm is getting tired and my pitch is losing its punch.

I can't say I'm disappointed when Annelise finally says her shoulder is feeling better. Next inning, Dad puts her on the pitcher's mound and moves me to center field. Annelise pitches like a champ despite her sore shoulder and chipped nail!

The Huskies get a few more runs, but so do we. Then Jenny hits a home run for the Huskies! But when we're at bat, so does Henry!

I can barely believe it, but by the final inning, the score is Huskies 4, Chihuahuas 5. *Woof, woof!* We're winning!

All we have to do is hold our lead. But the Huskies are up to bat. If they get one run in, the game is tied, two runs in and they remain the undefeated team in the league. If we can just keep them from scoring, we'll break their winning streak!

Annelise rubs her sore shoulder. She has to pitch like she's never pitched before.

"You can do it, Annelise!" I yell from center field as she faces the next batter.

Annelise glances over her shoulder at me. Then she reaches down and rubs a little dirt on her bright pink socks. I draw a good-luck smiley face with the toe of my cleat in the center-field grass.

Our good-luck charms must be working because Annelise strikes out the next two batters! Just one more out, and we will win the game.

Katie steps up to the plate. Unfortunately, she hits Annelise's first pitch.

BAM!

The ball tears deep into right field for a two-base hit. Now the Huskies have a runner on second base.

"You got this one, Annelise!" I yell from center field as the next batter steps up to the plate.

Then I see who it is.

¡Ay! It's Jenny!

Just like Henry, she hit a home run earlier in the game. I look at Dad to see if he tips his hat to Annelise, which is the signal to walk the batter on purpose so she doesn't have a chance to hit another home run. If Annelise walks her, Jenny will get on base, but at least we won't give her the chance to hit one out of the ballpark.

All eyes are on Dad. But instead of tipping his hat, he rubs his nose, which is the signal for *Strike 'er out!*

Annelise gives Dad a confident nod.

Henry repositions his feet behind the plate.

Jenny raises her bat.

I back up and get ready to catch a fly ball if she hits it to center field. Even though I want Jenny to do well, Annelise is on my team, so I want her to do even better.

Annelise glances back, checking on the base runners. She catches my eye again. I give her a winning smile. Then she takes a deep breath and turns to face the batter.

The next pitch is solid but low. Jenny should let it go by for a ball, but at the last moment, she gives the ball a hard chop. It skips across the dirt like a stone on water, straight down the center of the diamond — straight for Annelise.

Annelise crouches down and holds her glove to the ground, waiting for the ball to bounce in. But instead of landing in her glove, the ball takes an extra hop and hits Annelise, right in the face!

Chapter 11

Annelise Gets Her Crown

Annelise cries out in pain. She crumples to the ground as the ball rolls to a stop. Jenny freezes halfway to first base, staring at Annelise, but her mom hollers, "Run, Jenny!" She dashes to first base, but her eyes are on Annelise the whole time.

Henry rushes over and grabs the ball. The rest of us hurry to the mound and huddle around Annelise. She's hunched over, shoulders shaking, and tears gushing from her eyes. Her hand is cupping her mouth.

The umpire calls for a time-out as Dad breaks through our circle and kneels next to Annelise.

When he pulls her hand away to look at her mouth, everyone lets out a gasp. Her lip is swollen and bleeding. One of her front teeth is broken off!

"It's not so bad," Dad tells her in a soothing voice, even though it looks really bad to me. "The tooth didn't get knocked out . . . just chipped. The same thing happened to me in a game, once. My dentist put a crown on the tooth and fixed it up, good as new, see?" Dad taps one of his front teeth. I never knew it was capped with a crown! "Your dentist will fix up your tooth too."

"B-but it really hurts!" Annelise sobs, cupping her mouth again. She starts crying harder than ever.

Dad looks around our circle. "Does anyone have a stick of gum?"

"I do," Drew says, pulling a pack of bubblemint gum from his back pocket.

Dad takes a stick and works it between his fingers like a piece of clay. "The gum will protect your broken tooth and help with the pain," he reassures Annelise.

Annelise hesitates but then uncovers her mouth, letting Dad gently press the gum around her broken tooth, wrapping it up nice and snug. Tears and dust are mixing with the blood on Annelise's chin. Her fat lip is starting to bruise. She looks like a boxer who just stepped out of the ring, but no one, not even Henry, tells her that there's no crying in softball.

Actually, no one says much of anything at all. We just pat Annelise on the back and mumble things like, "You'll be okay," and, "Don't worry." Sometimes that's all a friend can do.

Annelise is still crying when Dad finishes with the gum, but a moment later she looks at him through her tears and says, "Thanks, Coach. It feels better now."

Dad helps Annelise to her feet. I feel more proud of him than I ever have before. I'm not a little kid any-more, but Dad is still my superhero.

Annelise's mom and dad rush over from the stands. They hug Annelise close, then lead her off the field. I can hear her dad on his phone, talking with someone at the dentist's office in town. When they get to the gate, the whole crowd stands up and applauds for Annelise.

I start to take off after her, but Dad puts his hand on my shoulder, stopping me. "Where are you going, Vicka?" he asks. "The game isn't over. We need a pitcher."

"B-b-but," I say, my voice choppy with tears. "I don't think I can."

Dad squeezes my shoulder again. "*I* do."

"So do we!" Bea adds. The rest of the team nods in agreement.

"Let's show 'em who's boss, Applesauce," Henry says, putting the ball in my hand.

Now everyone is patting *me* on the back saying things like, "Let's finish this thing," and, "We'll win it for Annelise."

As the crowd settles into their seats again, Dad sends Tony to center field. I head to the mound.

I give Henry my most confident nod even though I'm shaking from the top of my pink cap to the toes of my dusty cleats. I'm not as good at pitching as Annelise, but now the whole team is counting on me to keep the next batter from hitting the runners home and winning the game.

As Henry crouches down behind home plate, I take a deep breath and smooth out the dirt in front of me. Then I draw a dusty smiley face with the toe of my cleat. Dirty socks may bring Henry good luck, but smiles help *me* get by.

Henry pounds his fist into his mitt as we get ready for a few practice throws. "Right in the pocket, pitcher!" he shouts, holding up his mitt to make a target for me.

I look at Henry's mitt and imagine the softball smacking into it. Then I wind up for my first practice pitch and let the ball fly.

SLAM!

Henry grins with surprise. "Hot sauce!" he cries, throwing the ball back to me.

I take a few more practice pitches, then glance around the diamond. Runners on first and second.

Drew gives me a nod from third base. "You can do it, Vicka!" he shouts. "Just one more batter out, and we win!"

I smile at my crush, but on the inside I'm cringing. "Just two more runs and we lose," I mumble to myself. But I can't think about that now. I have to focus on winning the game for Annelise. For Dad. For all of us.

I take a deep breath and nod to the ump. She gets into position behind Henry. "Play ball!" she shouts.

I feel my knees wobble as the next Husky walks up to the plate.

It's Steamroller!

¡Uf!

Dad must know that I'm nervous because I hear him shout, "Take your time, Bonita! Nice and easy!"

I let Dad's words fill me up with courage. Then I line up my pitch. I grip the ball with my fingertips, just like Uncle Julio taught me. I wind up, just like I've done a million times before, and let the ball snap from my wrist.

It sizzles through the air. The pitch is perfect, but Steamroller watches it go by. He must want to see what I'm made of before he takes a swing.

The ball sinks into Henry's mitt.

"Strike one!" the ump shouts.

I threw a strike! My heart is doing a happy dance inside my chest, but I have to keep it together and stay focused. If Steamroller wants to see what I'm made of, I'll show him.

I pitch the ball again.

This time, Steamroller swings.

Whoosh!

"Steee-rike two!"

My head is spinning as Henry throws the ball back to me. "One more time, pitcher!" he shouts.

"You can do it, Vicka!" I hear Bea cry out from left field.

I catch Jenny's eye as she stands, ready to pounce for second base if I give her the chance. She wants to win the game as much as me. But she gives me a quick *go-for-it!* nod.

I smile to myself. We may be competitors today, but we are best friends always.

Turning back to face Steamroller, I wind up and pitch the ball, dead center.

Steamroller swings his bat hard and smashes the ball right down the middle of the diamond — right for me!

There's no time to think. I lift my glove and scrunch my eyes shut as I feel the ball slam against my hand. Quickly pulling my glove to my chest, I hesitate. Did the ball stay in or did it bounce out?

Opening my eyes again, I dare to look inside my glove. A bright yellow softball gleams back at me. I hold it up for all to see.

The crowd explodes with cheering. Our fans are on their feet!

The next thing I know, I'm being tackled by a pack of howling Chihuahuas! "We won! We won!"

Bea races in from left field and gives me a giant hug. Dad gives me a big smile. Drew and Henry lift me to their shoulders! Everyone dances around us cheering for our team.

If Annelise were here I would feel like the queen of the diamond. But I won't feel like a winner until I know she's okay.

Chapter 12

Queen of Diamonds

"Look out below!" Henry hollers. He cannonballs right into the pool where all the Pink Chihuahuas are splashing around. But we're not at the city pool tonight. After our big win against the undefeated Huskies earlier today, Dad offered to buy ice cream for everyone, like always. But instead of biking to Java Jane's, all of us — the Chihuahuas and even some of the Huskies, including Jenny, Katie and Grace — biked to the dentist office where Annelise's parents took her after the accident.

We all hung out in the parking lot, talking together and listening to Bea's playlist, until Annelise and her parents finally came out. Annelise was so surprised to see all of us there that she burst into tears all over again.

Her dad shook hands with everyone. Her mom gave all of us hugs. They told us Annelise would be fine, and her tooth would soon be fixed. Then Mr. Lane invited everyone to his house for a pool party. That's where we are now.

Bea's softball soundtrack is blasting from the patio speakers. Poco is sitting on a pink cushion, chewing a delicious doggie bone, like he is the prince of the party. Annelise is sitting next to him under a pool umbrella, even though it's a clear, starry night. She's wearing her Queen of Diamonds shirt and holding an ice pack on her mouth. Her lip is still swollen, but now her broken tooth is capped with a temporary crown, so she doesn't look so much like a hockey player anymore. She'll get a permanent crown in a couple weeks. Then she really will be crowned the queen of our team!

As I hop out of the water to take a dive off the board, Annelise calls me over to where she's sitting on her lounge chair. "Julia said you took over for me after I got hurt," she says, handing me a beach towel. "She said you were top dog on the pitcher's mound."

I wrap the towel around me and sit down next to Annelise. "I did okay, but I don't think the Chihuahuas have a top dog. I think we're just a pack of scrappy pups."

Annelise starts to smile, then winces. "Ouchies," she says, rubbing her jaw.

"Sorry to make you smile," I reply, which only makes her smile again.

"Who wants a burger?" Dad calls from across the patio. He's helping Mr. Lane grill hamburgers and hot dogs. Mom and some of the other parents brought chips, salads, and ice cream for dessert!

"Not me," Annelise says, cradling her mouth. "But I wouldn't mind some nice, soft ice cream. Chocolate, if you've got it."

"Coming right up!" Mom says, scooping chocolate ice cream into a bowl. Lucas brings it over to Annelise.

"Thanks, dog boy," she says patting my little brother on the head.

"I'm the ice cream boy now!" Lucas replies. Then goes back to help Mom scoop more.

Everyone starts getting in line for food.

Bea and Jenny rush up to us. "C'mon, besties!" Bea says to Annelise and me. "Let's eat!"

Annelise lifts her bowl. "I'll stick with ice cream for now," she says. Then she looks at Jenny. "Um . . . I'm sorry about the whole frenemy thing," she tells her. "It was nice of you, Katie, and Grace to come to the dentist's office, even though my team beat the paws off your team." Annelise holds her hand out to Jenny. "Friends?"

Jenny shakes hands with Annelise. "Friends," she says. "And I'm really sorry I chipped your tooth."

"*You* didn't chip it, the ball did," Annelise replies. "Besides, now I'll get to wear a crown . . . permanently!"

She shifts to a queenly pose, lifting her ice cream cone like a royal scepter.

The three of us giggle along with her. Annelise smiles at us, and this time she doesn't wince.

As Bea, Jenny, and I get in line for burgers, I look up into the night sky. Sure, my confidence gets rattled sometimes. I'll probably bobble again and again when life throws me more curveballs. But I'll keep playing the game and trusting my team to cheer me on.

I smile at the moon.

It's surrounded by a bunch of friendly stars.

Just like me.

About the Author

Julie Bowe lives in Mondovi, Wisconsin, where she writes popular books for children, including *My Last Best Friend*, which won the Paterson Prize for Books for Young People and was a Barnes & Noble 2010 Summer Reading Program book. In addition to writing for kids, she loves visiting with them at schools, libraries, conferences, and book festivals throughout the year.

Glossary

audition (aw-DISH-uhn)—a tryout performance for an actor or musician

cleats (KLEETS)—athletic shoes with spikes on the bottom to help grip dirt and grass playing fields

dugout (DUHG-out)—a low shelter holding the players' bench; softball diamonds have one dugout for each team

financial (fye-NANS-shuhl)—having to do with money

impersonation (im-PUR-suh-nay-shuhn)—to pretend to be someone else

plague (PLAYG)—a disease that spreads quickly and kills most people who catch it

register (REJ-uh-stur)—to enter someone or something on an official list

sacrifice (SAK-ruh-fise)—to give up something important or enjoyable for a good reason

scepter (SEP-tur)—a rod or staff carried by a king or queen as a symbol of authority

sincere (sin-SEER)—straightforward and honest

sponsor (SPON-sur)—a person or company that gives a team equipment or money in exchange for advertising

strategy (STRAT-uh-gee)—a careful plan to achieve a goal

volunteer (vol-uhn-TIHR)—a person who chooses to do work without pay

Time to Talk

Questions for you and your friends

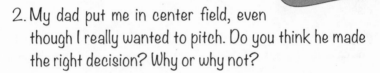

1. Annelise was surprisingly nice this summer during softball. How was she a good friend and teammate?

2. My dad put me in center field, even though I really wanted to pitch. Do you think he made the right decision? Why or why not?

3. Our team showed great sportsmanship throughout the softball season. What were some ways we stayed positive and encouraged one another?

4. At first, Annelise didn't want me talking to Jenny because she was on the other team. Do you think I should have listened to her? Why or why not?

Just for You

Writing prompts for your journal

1. Bea is always an optimist in any situation. I tend to look at the negative side of things. Are you more like Bea or me? Why?

2. I was excited and then nervous about my dad coaching my softball team. Has one of your family members ever coached your team? How did you feel about it?

3. Have you ever had to play a position in a sport that you didn't want to? How did you handle it?

4. In the book, I talk about how I see my parents differently now than I did when I was younger. How has your view of your parents changed from when you were younger?

Word to the Wise

Playing a team sport isn't always easy. Sometimes you win, sometimes you lose. Sometimes you will be the star of the game, sometimes it will be your biggest frenemy.

But no matter what, it's important to always stay positive and be a supportive team player. Here are a few tips on how to be a good team player:

How to be a good team player:

◊ Encourage and cheer on your teammates. Even if you are competing for a certain position, don't let the competition get in the way of supporting each other.

◊ Never put down a teammate when they make a mistake. That's just mean!

◊ Listen to your coach. He or she has a lot more experience than you do.

◊ Practice, practice, practice. It can only make you better, faster, and stronger!

◊ Always try your hardest. It's a waste of everyone's time if you don't.

◊ Don't put down the opposing team or players. Being rude to your opponents is just plain mean. Plus, being in sports is a great way to meet all kinds of new people from all over.

Cooking Corner

After reading about all of those postgame ice cream treats, I bet you want your own! But did you know that *you* can make your own ice cream?

DELICIOUS HOMEMADE ICE CREAM

INGREDIENTS

2 Tbsp. sugar

1 cup half-and-half

1 tsp. vanilla extract

½ cup coarse salt

ice

EQUIPMENT

spoon

medium bowl

pint-sized Ziplock bag

gallon-sized Ziplock bag

1. In medium bowl, combine sugar, vanilla, and half-and-half. Pour mixture into a pint-sized bag.

2. Fill a gallon-sized bag half full of ice and pour salt on top.

3. Put the sealed pint-sized bag into the gallon-sized bag and seal tightly.

4. Shake the bags for five minutes. Continue shaking until the ice cream is hard.

5. Rinse the salt off the pint-sized bag, and enjoy your homemade ice cream! For harder ice cream, put the bag in the freezer until firm.

MIX-IT-UP IDEAS

- For a different flavor, try adding strawberry, chocolate, or caramel syrup instead of vanilla.

- Throw in some sprinkles, nuts, or pretzels to add a little crunch to your ice cream.

- A few drops of food coloring will brighten up your ice cream.

Victoria Torres

Unfortunately Average

Always Looking for her way to shine!

When bossy Annelise insists on making the school fund-raiser a stuffy formal, the rest of the committee worries that the boys won't go and the fund-raiser will be a flop. Victoria Torres suggests they trade tiaras for cowboy hats and make the dance a Wild West theme. Annelise finally agrees but on one condition: they make it a Sadie Hawkins dance where the girls ask the boys. Will Victoria find the nerve to ask her crush Drew to the dance, or will she remain the most unfortunately average chicken around?

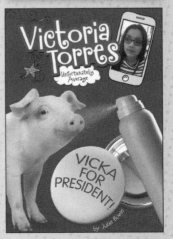

Find out more about Victoria's
unfortunately average life, plus
get cool downloads and more at

www.capstonekids.com

(Fortunately, it's all fun!)